The Book of Jobe

James West

This is a work of fiction.

ISBN: 9781087112756

Chapter 1

Mark Chase was in the zone. This was his church, his hour of meditation. He'd ridden his motorcycle down the freeway to Ortega Highway and carefully maneuvered through the residential neighborhoods until the road opened up and headed toward the mountains. Now, as the midmorning sun crested the hills, he began winding his way to the top where he'd have a cup of coffee and chat with the boys before heading home at a leisurely pace with just enough time to shower, change, and take his wife to lunch. He felt good and he looked good. The morning chill had worn off, so he unzipped his new leather jacket about three inches to allow some airflow. He thought about buying new gloves as he worked his hands, the freeway ride was a bit cold for his thin gloves. He hadn't considered cold weather riding gear when he first bought the bike, assuming that Sunday drives up and down the coast would be the majority of his riding time. With this new Sunday routine of mountain riding, he alternated between being too cold in the early morning freeway run, and too hot when he returned around noon. At the suggestion of a new friend he'd met at the top of the hill, he'd bought a pair of jeans that had Kevlar woven into the fabric. They had better safety while still looking casual. Mark loved good design.

As the road began to twist and turn, he leaned first this way, then the other, a little faster than the speed limit, but never crossing the line, always in control. It had become a ritual, every Sunday morning for the last six months. He loved the fluid way his body and the machine worked as one unit. It freed his mind from the stress of a hectic schedule.

He decelerated ever so slightly, leaned to his left and gently rolled on the throttle through the apex of the corner, shifting his body at the exit to set up for the upcoming right-hand bend of the familiar "S" turn. On the opposite side of the road, facing him, a car had pulled off at the turnout. There was no reason for concern. The car was stopped, and well off the road on the opposite side, probably taking in the view for a minute before continuing down the hill. As Mark straightened and then leaned into the right-hand turn, the car abruptly accelerated. It was pointing straight at him, but there was no reason to expect the driver would do anything other than enter his own lane and continue down the road. Except, it didn't. It continued to accelerate directly toward him.

Mark was committed to the turn. He could lean it in harder, which would put him directly into the hillside. If he straightened the bike up, he'd go head first into their windshield, and if he was lucky enough that his body cleared the car, it would go plunging down the embankment. He had no choice but to hold his line and pray that the other driver got his car under control and back into his own lane. The car continued to accelerate in a straight line.

The outside corner of the bumper hit his left foot hard. "Oh, that's gonna hurt," was the thought that flashed through his mind when he felt the impact. His boots were made to protect his feet and ankles from road surface in the event of a crash. There was no riding gear on earth that would protect him from the direct impact of a three thousand pound vehicle. The motorcycle immediately straightened as the rear end pitched out to his right. The forces launched his butt from the seat, and in slow motion he was looking down at the top of the gas tank while his body sailed through the air.

His brain took it all in during that split second, time slowed to a crawl, and for a moment he was back in engineering class, drawing angled lines with arrows indicating the direction of force: Vector 1 - 35mph, Vector 2 - force of gravity opposite the angle of lean, Vector 3 - object of impact traveling at unknown speed, Vector 4 - direction of the projectile - his body. Mark knew instinctively that if he cleared the embankment, he would land in the middle of the road at the exit of the blind corner. He hoped there wasn't a car coming from the other direction.

His forward motion of approximately 35 miles per hour was stopped abruptly when the right side of his body hit a tree just shy of the embankment, then fell to the ground like a fork-full of spaghetti. The motorcycle, after having propelled him forward like a catapult, followed behind along that same vector of force until it was stopped by the same tree. It came to a rest on top of Mark's body. Force equals mass times acceleration. It is measured in newtons, which can be converted to pressure, which in turn can be expressed as a dependent variable of the surface area of the body where it contacts the tree. But the laws of physics don't really matter when you're no longer part of the physical world.

The object of impact traveling at an unknown speed had stopped its forward motion in the middle of the street. The driver, having witnessed the wondrous mechanics of the physical world as it functioned within the boundaries of Albert's theories, looked over their left shoulder at the results. Satisfied, they took their foot off the brake pedal, turned the wheel, and sped down the mountain. Mark watched as it drove away. He was confused and didn't fully appreciate what had just happened. Looking around, he wondered where he was, and how he had gotten there. He wasn't in pain. It felt very strange, but he was warm and comfortable. Looking down, he saw the mangled Triumph lying atop a lifeless body. "Is that *me*?" he wondered.

Chapter 2

When the radio alarm clicked on, Robert Jobe rolled over and listened to the music. It was playing the Rufus Wainwright version of Leonard Cohen's Hallelujah. As the third verse rounded the corner toward the chorus he joined Rufus out loud with "It's a cold and it's a broken Hallelujah." As the melancholic tune ambled on, Robert reached out and hit the snooze bar for ten more minutes of painlessness.

After a second snooze he rolled out of bed and tested the floor, first stretching his calves, then standing, making sure his knee held firm. In the darkness of the unlit bathroom he fished two aspirin out of the bottle, the blind habit becoming almost routine, and turned the shower on full hot. Swallowing the meds, he mumbled to himself "breakfast of champions" and stepped into the hot spray, feeling his muscles loosen and his blood begin to flow.

He surfed the news channels over a cup of coffee. Flipping from the home invasion where an elderly couple was killed in their bed, to the school bus that overturned while the driver was texting, to the mangled car of the drunk driver that managed to get broadsided by an oak tree. He finally settled on a human-interest story. A man had invented a way to protect his small dogs from the coyotes that were increasingly making their way from the foothills into the backyards of unsuspecting suburbanites. "How would we entertain ourselves," he thought, "if it weren't for death, destruction and desperation."

Finishing his coffee, Robert strapped on a knee brace and carefully maneuvered the pant leg of his old off-brand work jeans over it. He laced on a pair of low ankle hiking boots and shrugged into his heavy jacket. He took one last lingering look at the cane by the door before deciding to go without. The boots weren't so good for walking, but the walks were making him stronger. The healing process seemed agonizingly slow. In the pre-sun early morning darkness, he carefully negotiated the wooden staircase along the side of the garage over which his little apartment hideaway was perched. As he walked, the early morning cold began to seep through his clothes. The cold in Southern California was milder than what he was used to in New Mexico, but it was wetter here and he felt it more severely. He knew that his jacket would be way too heavy for the afternoon and evening sun. He picked up the pace and his body heat quickly began to fight against the damp. Halfway down the second block, a jogger came up from behind, slowed, and fell into step.

Initially, Robert didn't react in any way; he just kept pace as they walked together. Finally turning his head, Robert saw that his new companion was a good foot taller than he, and half again as wide, with broad shoulders and large hands. His sweat pants and hooded pullover were well worn, but he was running with a new pair of Nike high tops. Robert couldn't see the man's face.

A few blocks ahead of them, an early model Japanese sedan turned out of an alley and onto the street heading in their direction. It had been modified with lower and stiffer suspension than the stock version. The windows had been tinted and the exhaust was deep and throaty, indicating an aftermarket performance upgrade. As it drew nearer the two men, it slowed.

The jogger straightened as he walked, and without breaking stride he reached up and slid the hood of his sweatshirt back off his head. Robert noticed that the smooth black skin covering the baldhead was pulled tight across the man's face and made a gentle slope down his neck widening the attachment of head to shoulder. The man obviously lifted weights as well as jogged. The driver of the little car downshifted and accelerated past the two on foot.

After the car sped past, Robert looked up at the profile walking by his side. He'd never seen this man before, but when the face turned toward him the crystal-clear gray eyes were instantly recognizable.

"Michael! Robert huffed. "I don't need your protection."

"I go where I'm sent."

"Tell him to leave me alone. Tell him I'll take my chances."

"It doesn't work that way."

"It seems to work that way for everybody else!" Robert contested.

"It's not your place to ask why," Michael said, "and I'm not a messenger."

They walked the remainder of the block in silence. As they neared the crosswalk, Michael put his hood up and turned down the side street continuing his jog. Robert watched as the lone runner passed under the first streetlight. He waited, but never saw him emerge from the shadows to pass under the second streetlight. Robert turned in the opposite direction and crossed the street to a little breakfast diner. Sitting at the counter, he watched the light bathe the streets outside as he ate. The traffic picked up and the sun came out and soon it was time to head to work.

Exiting the diner, Robert saw a man sitting cross legged with a guitar in his lap, his back against the outer wall. The handwritten sign in the guitar case said "hungry." The man's clothes were dirty and sun bleached having lost all color. Robert stopped and reached into his pocket. The single loose bill he pulled out was a twenty and without hesitation he dropped it into the case and said, "have a hot breakfast."

The man picked up the money and turned to look at him. His face and hands were a dusty brown, heavily tanned and wrinkled. At first, Robert couldn't tell if the man was in his twenties or his forties, then his eyes turned from brown to a deep piercing blue.

"You're a good man," he said, "blameless and upright, and the Lord will restore all that you've lost."

Robert could feel the anger rising up and he clenched his jaw tight.

"GABRIEL!" He blurted out, just a little too loudly. "Tell him no thanks, don't do me any favors."

The man's eyes stayed their shade of blue and held Robert's gaze. Finally, the man spoke again: "You are to be restored greater than before."

"Don't speak to me of restoration! He should have thought about my reaction before he took my family," Robert said, barely containing his emotion. "I'm broken. You can repair a broken lamp, but it will never become unbroken. Some things can't be unremembered. My joy is gone and I wish to remember the way it was, not have it replaced. Why take them and leave me? It should have been the other way around. It was cruel, there is nothing left to restore. He should have swept up the pieces of me and discarded them properly. Instead, he glues me back together and puts me on a shelf? He expects me to shine with the same light as before? No thanks! Better that I'd never been born. His destruction was too complete. He didn't just break my body, he broke my spirit."

"You're the one that asked to be His instrument."

"Instrument yes, *tool* no."

Robert turned his back on the man and headed up the sidewalk. No one noticed the man's eyes turn from blue to brown as he stood with the money and walked into the diner. Furious, Robert was counting the cracks in the sidewalk as he went. At thirty-three, his anger began to fade. He had walked two city blocks by the time he stopped to look around. Across the street, sunbeams were piercing the treetops that lined the park. They burned holes in the mist, which danced in circles around the deadly shafts of light. The mist seemed happy as it gladly succumbed its physical bindings, changing form, and dissipating into the heated air.

"Why not me?" He thought as he watched the water change form. "Why can't I just close my eyes and vaporize?" He closed his eyes and raised his arms into the air. Bowing his head, he looked like a man in church giving praise as he felt the sun warm the back of his neck. When Robert opened his eyes again he was alone on the sidewalk. Even the mist in the park was gone. "Why must I endure?" He said aloud to no one in particular.

Robert looked around at the new morning that he'd been blessed to witness one more time. The sun was warm and there was a cool, light breeze. The sky was bright blue and contrasted with puffy white clouds. People were smiling, walking, driving, and talking on their phones. He took a deep breath and shook his head as he let it out.

"Another beautiful, perfect, glorious, god damned day!" He said to himself as he continued his walk to work. He used to have a catchphrase that all his employees knew him by: "Every breath is a gift." These days, it seemed, every breath carried with it both a blessing and a curse.

Chapter 3

"I wish this meeting were taking place in a more formal environment," the man in the dark blue suit turned his head toward his drinking companion and smiled, "like the golf course."

Eric Pierce swirled his scotch and soda and motioned to the bartender for another. "I don't golf," he said.

"All the better! I like to bet when I play."

"I'm not a betting man," Eric said without a smile.

They were standing at the bar of a high-end restaurant in Newport Beach. The bar was dark mahogany with maroon booths. In the mirror over the bar they could see the expanse of the modest dining room that led to the open patio overlooking the harbor. The dining area had beautifully sculpted trees in large wooden pots. The trees were strung with tiny white lights. The lights played on the water that trickled down the three-dimensional sculptures which were tastefully placed around the restaurant.

"Based on what you just proposed, you couldn't convince me you're not a betting man."

Eric was nervous and trying hard not to show it. The meeting was a long-shot gamble, but with the recent turn of events his options were dwindling. He needed to create a new opportunity, so he reached out to one of their larger corporate partners, contacting their Chief Financial Officer and arranged to meet and discuss his idea. Eric believed their respective positions made them peers. Now, standing in the man's presence, Eric was physically uncomfortable, in contrast to his counterpart.

Upon entering the bar Eric thought nothing of it, having had dinner here before once or twice. He considered the place snooty and overpriced, but it was fun to spend the evening in a beautiful atmosphere on special occasions. When the CFO entered the bar, he immediately started shaking hands and greeting people on a first name basis and Eric knew he'd been lured to the other man's home turf. "Strike one," he thought to himself.

In closer proximity, after shaking hands and ordering drinks, Eric became acutely aware of clothes. It was the silly little things that unnerved him sometimes. He felt his body temperature rise and his armpits begin to sweat. While the CFO chatted with the bartender like they were old friends, being handed his usual without having to order it, Eric took measure of the man: His suit was custom tailored, his white shirt monogrammed on the cuffs, and his red silk tie was a designer brand. Eric's suit was off the rack. His shirts didn't fit as well as he wanted, either they were loose around the neck and correct in the sleeves, or correct in the neck and short in the sleeves. Today, he'd opted for a loose neck, looking for that stylish half-inch of shirtsleeve to exit his jacket correctly. He felt outclassed and chided himself for not having enough cash in his wallet to pay for their drinks. That was strike two in his mind.

"Look," Eric began, "Chase Industries is in a crisis." He was trying to invalidate the "betting man" comment and turn his adversary into an ally. "We both know that the Japanese word for crisis has the same meaning as opportunity. I'm just trying to capitalize on a bad situation. It wasn't intended, but it is what it is."

The CFO was instantly irritated. He had very little tolerance for stupidity and was beginning to question his decision to meet with this joker. He hated the phrase "it is what it is" almost as much as when his kids would try to end an argument by making the claim "same difference". He couldn't afford to walk away from the meeting quite yet, however, since it was possible the proposal could actually germinate into something worth cultivating, and he would be remiss to ignore it. But he couldn't ignore the "door" the man just kicked open, so he decided to walk through it. He considered it a test, maybe the joker would reply with "same difference" and he could simply turn and walk away.

"Actually, it's the Chinese word for crisis that you're referring to, not Japanese. And even that's not correct. It's a myth of Western business gurus and motivational speakers. The Chinese characters can't be separated and taken as literal translations into English." The CFO took a drink and waited for a response.

Eric's face turned red but he didn't respond. "Fair enough" the man thought, and continued:

"You say *capitalize* on a bad situation. It could be interpreted as an attempt to *take advantage* in the aftermath of a tragedy. The whole proposal could cast an ugly shadow on all involved. Tell me sir: Are you a shameless opportunist? Or do you truly believe that your suggestion may be in the best interest of everyone? Are you close enough to know her mindset? This is a very difficult time for her, which means you are in a delicate situation. You need to be careful."

"I AM careful. I will be careful. Are you interested or not?" Eric was losing his patience. He was clearly being patronized.

The CFO took another sip and gazed into the harbor. His boat was in a slip just outside the restaurant. He loved his boat. He'd put a flag on the highest mast so that he could see it from the bar. He counted the masts from the closest slip until he hit seven and saw his little flag rocking side to side ever so gently. It made him feel good about himself. The joker didn't need to know he owned a boat. Originally, he thought he might invite him aboard, but after meeting the man he'd decided against it. Now he was kicking himself that he'd even suggested meeting at his favorite restaurant. He downed the rest of his drink and thought that if he handled this correctly, hopefully he would never see this man again.

"Of course we're interested," he told Eric. "It's a shame that the world has lost Mark Chase's genius, but life goes on. Chase has manufacturing rights for two years, after that time the manufacturing contract for his design will be a competitive bid across multiple suppliers. It would be in our best interest to own the patent, but the impact is minimal so it's not a critical factor. Here's what I recommend: You take the lead and get it on the table. We can't be formally involved until it comes from Chase to us. If it comes to us, we'll consider it. But let's not meet again. Any further communication needs to come through official channels."

"If I can put this together I'd expect to be compensated," Eric jumped in quickly, continuing the conversation so that his counterpart wouldn't walk out and stick him with the bill. "What I mean is, I hope to have more control at Chase, but I should also be part of architecting the merger. If I can make this happen, I'll expect a significant option on the transaction."

With that comment, the CFO knew in his bones that the deal wouldn't happen. In fact, it made him feel sorry for the guy. He'd met Mark Chase, and was certain that the Chase lawyers would conduct business properly and not allow this guy to "double dip" no matter what his position within the company. And he doubted very much that anyone with real power at Chase Industries would stoop to make deals under the table. Looking out across the restaurant and into the harbor, he calculated that in another year he could afford to get out of Newport and make the move to La Jolla. But would his wife make the move? She loved it here in South Orange County. If he could convince her, he could leave work and be drinking martinis off the back of his boat in thirty minutes, instead of spending an hour and a half in traffic.

"Of course!" The executive said encouragingly, and tossing a twenty on the bar he added, "Everyone should be compensated according to the value of his or her contribution." He walked out and handed the valet his ticket. While he waited, he absentmindedly brushed a spec of lint off the shoulder of his Italian suit. It was a minute symbolic gesture, but with it he felt the weight of his meeting with Eric Pierce lift from his shoulders and comfort in knowing he'd probably never cross paths with the man in the future. When the Mercedes drove up, and the door was held open, he felt good about himself again.

Chapter 4

Hurting worse than normal, Robert questioned the wisdom of not using his cane for almost a week. Changes in barometric pressure seemed to have an adverse effect on his damaged joints and on this particular morning the air was thick with moisture.

"Bob Job!" Joey called from the back of the shop as Robert came through the door. He stopped in his tracks and glared at the young man.

"I know, I know, I'm sorry," Joey said as he came forward, his hands raised with palms out in supplication. "I couldn't help myself. Look! We got a motorcycle job! Some guy dropped it off this morning and says he's looking for an old-school custom."

Robert saw the wreck of a late model Triumph Bonneville. It looked pretty broken up, but Robert had a soft spot for British twins, and after making a couple of laps around the motorcycle he was already starting to formulate what he might keep and where he might go with the design.

Joey was bouncing on the balls of his feet, eager to start on a new project. Robert tended to refer to Joey as "the kid" in response to Joey's calling him an "old man." They were only about twenty years apart, Joey in his twenties and Robert in his forties, but their differences were notable: Joey still had the exuberance of youth, ready and willing to take on the world. Robert felt twenty years older than his body, with aches and pains to match, and experiences he wouldn't wish upon the worst of enemies.

"Old-school meaning what exactly?" Robert asked.

"I'm not sure, the guy says he'll be back later in the week to discuss the design. I'm figuring full chopper, you know: Captain America style. Raked front forks, hard tail, ape hanger bars, the whole shebang." Joey was very excited. He'd been the lead metal fabricator at the shop for the last couple years and all he talked about was custom motorcycles. Ken, the owner of the shop, made a living with whatever walked through the door. That sometimes meant replacing rusted out floor pans and side panels for automotive restoration. But more often than not, it meant decorative pieces and trim for the gated communities of the high rent district.

"That's not old-school," Robert told him, "that's late 60's, early 70's."

"That's before I was born!" Joey contested. "What were *you* thinking?"

"I'm thinking 40's and 50's," Robert pondered the idea and started pointing as he circled the mangled pile of bike parts. "Keep the rake like it is, remove any unnecessary body parts, and put some thick, heavy tread tires front and back. We could add dirt track style handlebars, rubber boots around the forks, bring the pipes up a little and wrap them, make it a cross between a dirt tracker and a road bike. The original *old school* guys were focused on light and fast. It was an era just prior to the cafe racer. Post World War Two custom bobber: That's the style I'd go with; this bike's got Steve McQueen written all over it. Very cool if you do it right."

Joey had a look that was both questioning and disappointed. He'd wanted to get into custom builds and had been pushing Ken, the owner of the shop, to take on some side jobs. He'd even confided to Robert that he tried to get a job at one of the more prominent builders in the area. The beach towns of South Orange County were a hotbed of hot rodding since the early 60's, but they'd become a mecca of the custom automotive scene ever since Chip Foose got his television show. It was not an easy market to break into, and Ken wasn't interested in fame, he just wanted to pay his bills.

"Tell you what," Robert said, sensing the young man's disappointment, "find some photos on the internet of what you're thinking. I'll start to strip this thing down. Depending on what we've got left to work with, and of course the guy's budget, we'll come up with a couple variations. But keep two things in mind: One, we give the customer what he wants. Two, and for you this is more important, let's not just copy a design that one of the other shops might do. If you want to be a bike builder you've got to find your own style, otherwise you'll forever be just the guy that works the English Wheel."

That did the trick. Robert could see it in Joey's face: A sense of purpose. It immediately made Robert feel both energized, and old. Thinking back, he wondered: "When was the last time I felt like that?" He couldn't remember. After the accident he'd lost heart. He lost his family, he lost his friends, and he lost his business. He'd lost his joy. His faith had been heavily shaken, but he never lost hope. All he wanted to do now was get back to his roots and try to start over on his own terms.

He'd survived the accident, but didn't know why he was spared. He'd survived the operations, but had come to wish he hadn't. Therapy allowed him to walk again, but to where, and for what purpose? He'd packed what little he had left and went west to San Diego. With his background, he could easily have picked up a design job in the defense industry. Instead, he picked up a torch. It had been almost thirty years since he had learned to weld, and back then he loved it all: The fire, the forge, working with his hands, fixing stuff, making stuff. The thought had crossed his mind that "maybe, just maybe," he could once again find his passion.

The reality was much more difficult than he imagined. Motivation was a long time coming. For months he didn't want to get out of bed, but forced himself to take classes and relearn his craft using the new technologies that were available. Stick, TIG, MIG, it all came flooding back to him as naturally as riding a bicycle. Where he felt most comfortable, however, was gas welding and brazing finely detailed items. It took all his concentration and allowed him to escape his thoughts. Eventually, he became aware of the fact that he didn't want *to think*, he only wanted *to do*, and found that making small sculptures and jewelry gave him not only that opportunity, but also a way to get by financially. It was enough, at least, for him to keep putting one foot in front of the other as the days rolled on.

He'd met Ken, the owner of the shop, through the friend of a friend of an acquaintance. Ken took a look at his work and offered to buy lunch. Ken was a welder by trade and owned the little shop in Costa Mesa. During lunch, he confided with Robert that an illness in the family was making it hard for him to fulfill contracts. A deal was struck where Robert would have a place to live, over the garage in one of Ken's rental properties, close to the shop. It was a win-win: Robert would have steady work and still have time to pursue his art projects. Ken would be able to keep the shop open and maintain his income while freeing up the time needed to care for his family. The arrangement suited Robert just fine since neither intended it to be permanent.

As Ken entered the back of the shop Robert looked up from his work and called to him:

"How's the boy?"

Ken took a deep breath before answering:

"His spirits are up. One more chemo treatment tomorrow and he can come home for a month. The doctors tell us that the treatments are meeting their expectations. For now, at least," he paused for another breath. "Everything is going according to plan, but Judy is having a pretty rough time."

Robert knew that Judy wasn't the only one having a rough time. He could see the pain in Ken's face, and he knew all too well the feelings of desperation and fear. Child cancer. Shit happens. For the doctors at the hospital, it was just another day of effort and learning. For Ken, it was just another day of watching his life crumble to pieces and get washed out to sea, while all he could do was helplessly watch and wonder. Robert knew the feeling, and none of it made any sense to him. It made him hurt. It made him sad. It made him angry. Of all the strange twists of fate, an otherwise healthy child contracting cancer was one thing that Robert just couldn't wrap his mind around. It was not okay.

"What's this?" Ken asked, having caught sight of the motorcycle parts.

"New job apparently," Robert told him. "The kid's really excited about it," he said, smiling and nodding his head in Joey's direction. "We'll work it. You don't have to worry about it. I'll make sure it doesn't get out of hand."

Ken nodded appreciatively as he looked at the piles of motorcycle parts that Robert had been disassembling and separating. Suddenly, he pointed, and with a bit of concern in voice exclaimed: "I know this bike! Who brought it in?"

"Joey!?" Robert called.

"Who brought this in?" Ken asked as the younger man came forward from the back of the shop where he was hammering a design into a sheet of mild steel. He seemed a little apprehensive, wondering if maybe he was in some type of trouble.

"A young guy, maybe thirty? Said he picked it up at a police auction. I wrote up an invoice for quote-only and put it on your desk. I didn't want to send him away?"

"No, no, that's fine," Ken reassured him. "I think I recognize this bike, that's all. You guys keep working it. The phone number is on the invoice?"

Joey nodded. Ken turned and walked into the office, closing the door behind him. Robert turned and looked at Joey. Joey raised his eyebrows and returned to his anvil at the workbench along the back wall.

Chapter 5

"I'm sorry about all this Val. I know it feels like it's too soon, but there's never going to be a good time, and decisions need to get made."

They were sitting on the patio overlooking rolling hills of brown and green with the Pacific Ocean in the distance. Valerie Chase stared off toward the horizon. She was wearing a light blue sundress with yellow flowers. She'd grown tired of wearing black over the last six weeks, even though it still fit her mood. Changing her wardrobe and taking meetings on the patio was her attempt to move forward. "One step at a time," she thought. She wasn't ready to plunge head first into business matters, but she knew it was necessary, and she'd felt her husband's presence around her, urging her, like a small child tugging on her sleeve. Their lawyer, Tom Lawson, was there on her request. He'd come directly from his law office and was still wearing his wool suit. She wasn't ready, but it was time. "The business of life," her husband would say, "always needs tending."

After twenty-five years of marriage, this was the last thing she ever expected. Papers were spread across the glass top of the outdoor patio table. She looked down and carefully arranged them into four piles. If Mark were going over these documents with her, they would all be neatly bound into those file folders that had metal tangs at the top. They would all be in chronological order. He would walk her through them one by one, meticulously discussing the order in which they were developed, and why they were necessary. None of the piles took her by surprise except one. She was her husband's number one confidant; he kept nothing from her and often came to her for an opinion on their business matters. They had been partners in life, and business, since their first little apartment in Santa Ana. Over the last twenty years, they'd grown the business from a one-man operation where she handled the accounts, to hundreds of employees at their current location in Irvine. Their personal lives followed the same path of calculated and conservative steps all the way to the top of the hill where they currently lived overlooking the Newport Coast.

"Take your coat off Tom. Would you like more coffee?" Val asked as she retreated into the kitchen. Happy to oblige, he hung his jacket over the patio chair next to him as she refreshed both their cups. Val sat, took a sip of coffee, drew in a deep breath, and addressed her lawyer:

"Okay, run it by me again, slowly, stack by stack."

"Well, like I said, financially you're all set. The life insurance alone should cover all your needs for many years. If you're savvy with your investments, possibly even the rest of your life. Over the last year, Mark and Eric and I worked on a lot of other details. I don't know what prompted him…"

"I do," she cut him off, but didn't elaborate.

"Okay," he paused for a second before continuing, "in the last few months he had me file for a new patent."

"I'm aware of that," she said very matter of fact.

"He had me put all of his designs and licensing agreements into one corporate structure, separate, but of course connected via licensing, to the manufacturing operations."

"I'm aware of that also," she told him, "we were

compartmentalizing the assets ahead of a few contract proposals."

"Okay, and as I'm sure you're aware, you have complete ownership and control over those assets. Now the *plant*..."

The word hit her hard. It was her husband's term for their manufacturing facility. When Tom said it, it carried too much of Mark with it for her not to react. He used the term more than anyone; it was a term his father always used, having worked in the defense industry during its heyday in Orange County.

Upon hearing it, Val's emotions took a nostalgic trip down memory lane. Most of the defense firms had left the area over the years. Some still had operations in San Diego, and others kept their facilities near LAX, but the majority had moved their headquarters to a more tax-friendly state. After listening to his father's stories most of his life, Mark had made the decision to steer clear of military contracts as they built their business, choosing to focus on commercial products. It turned out to be a smart move. Technology had changed with lightning speed and most of the advances, and the money, had taken place in the consumer markets. It was only during the last few years that military spending had shifted enough for Mark to consider entertaining proposals. A drone manufacturer in San Diego had been doing quite well, and there was an opportunity to bid as a subcontractor for part of the mechanical structures. It was Mark's newest design, his latest patent, and it had won them that contract. It was a warm and friendly memory, but is was bittersweet. It came with a sadness that was still too ever present.

"I'm sorry, I missed that last part," she told Tom.

"The plant has equity ownership across all the employees," he continued. "You're still the majority shareholder, so all decisions need to go through you. Eric is part of the second-tier group of shareholders, being the comptroller and one of Mark's original employees. The rest of the share options are divided up across the other employees based on their classification. All of this got executed, but none of it has been communicated yet. None of your employees know, not even

Eric."

"I'm well aware of all these details." She told her lawyer. Not meaning for it to sound as abrupt as it came out, her tone stopped Tom Lawson short.

"We have plenty of money.' She continued in a softer tone. "Mark and I decided it was time to start giving back, and he felt the first place to start was with the people that helped us grow the business over the years. Keep going."

"These are the existing contracts and pending contracts," Tom said, placing his hand on the third stack of papers. "Pending contract proposals are all in order, no surprises there, they're only needing your signature. What's important here is the management structure. All of these contracts, existing and pending, need reassurance that Mark's death won't upset the apple cart."

"Rachael can take over. Mark had a lot of faith in her. I have a lot of faith in her. He'd been grooming her to step up. I don't see a problem."

"She's awful young," Tom Lawson cautioned.

"She's not that young. And she's a brilliant designer. She might not like the idea much, but I know her, she'll hit the ground running. She'll do fine."

"You'll need to make the announcement. But I still want to caution you; there's an old boys club associated with the majority of these contracts. They'll want to know that manufacturing will not be disrupted. They might respect your decision. Hell, they might even know Rachael. But one thing is certain; as far as they know, she has no proven track record for running a company. This is a matter of comfort and appearances. They might give her the time to prove herself, or they might pull their contracts. There's a couple that will probably take that route no matter what you decide."

"Understood," Val said, "let me think about it."

"Of course. Now, this last stack is preliminary fact finding and additional information regarding a buyout that Eric was negotiating."

"This is the one I don't understand," Val told him, it was the reason she wanted to walk through all the details a second time. "Mark would never consider this, and Eric doesn't have the authority to negotiate anything without Mark's involvement. And Mark wasn't involved. He would have told me. And why would he have set up the employee ownership structure if he intended to sell out?"

"I know. I wasn't aware of it either. Eric brought the file to me only last week."

"This makes no sense Tom." Val was angry, but she was very good at not showing it. "We ran this business as a team for ten years. Mark brought Eric into the company to handle the finances when we both felt it was important for me to become more active in the community.

"After we moved to Irvine I took on the role of public relations and stepped away from the finances, but that doesn't mean I wasn't involved. It was Mark's idea for me to get involved in charities, keep tabs on the planning commission, attend functions like hospital openings… It was a good strategy. Social networking helped us transition away from being a small business. And it helped us develop a solid reputation in the community.

"Does this file contain more than just fact finding and due diligence? Did someone approach him? Or, god forbid, did he reach out to somebody on his own? Do you know who he's been talking to and what they've been discussing?"

"I don't know," Tom conceded. "I can shut him down if you want."

"Why did you bring it to me at all?"

"When Eric brought it to me, he said it was another option that needed to be considered. I had a responsibility Val."

Valerie Chase pondered the stack of papers in front of her. Tom Lawson knew her well enough to stay quiet and allow her to think.

"Did Mark ever talk to you about Eric?" She asked finally, after what felt to Tom like a small eternity.

"A little. Not much. When we had lunch together, which wasn't all that often, he always laughed and referred to Eric's suggestions as the '*idea of the month*'. He liked Eric I think, but Mark was his own man. He had final say in any decision and

Eric knew that. I don't think Eric would have acted alone."

"You're right, Mark did like Eric. He appreciated his ambition and all his *'creative thinking'* as Mark used to call it. Mark was very careful not to give Eric too much slack. Mark kept me very much involved; he had me review all the financial reports. This company belongs to my husband and me, and we ran it together, no matter how we made it look to the outside world." She stopped to let that sink in with her lawyer. Tom nodded his understanding.

"Did he tell you he was thinking of replacing Eric?"

That took Tom by surprise. He thought about it for a few minutes before replying.

"Not exactly," Tom began, still sifting through his memory looking for clues, "I mean, not explicitly. Some of the meetings that took place over this last year, while we were architecting," he paused, "whatever strategy you were putting in place, I know it didn't include Eric specifically. I didn't think of it at the time. I just assumed it was Mark and Eric that were working the details together and his absence didn't indicate confidentiality. As we put together the equity agreement, Mark had me hire an accounting firm to run a series of valuations. You know, comparing salaries and positions, weighted by years of service. That sort of thing. I just assumed Mark had me take it outside because Eric had a vested interest and Mark wanted the final arrangement to be impartial."

"Did you ever mention any of this to Eric?"

"No, the opportunity never came up." The question surprised Tom. "You know I'm not full time staff. Mark would call me and we'd meet. Eric would never contact me directly, he knew better than to do that, the first thing I'd have done was call Mark," he told her with a shrug.

"It wouldn't matter either way," Val said reassuringly, "whether or not Eric knew. It's just very curious that's all." She shook her head. "But with Mark gone I need to fill you in on the details. Going outside the firm was my idea. You know Mark, 'solid ground' was one of his catchphrases. He was very conservative. Every time Eric brought him some new idea, Mark would say 'stick to the core business' and send him along gently. A year ago, we decided to rearrange a lot of things." Tom was nodding his agreement. "Mark felt that when we announced the equity arrangement, it would only be fair to give people the opportunity to leave without losing money. He didn't like the idea of locking someone in financially if they really didn't want to stay. So, key people were going to get their equity share either way. Eric was one of those key people. Mark was pretty sure Eric would leave if he had the opportunity." She paused in case her lawyer had questions.

"Okay," Tom said with a shrug, "so Eric's position was good either way. He had the freedom to choose at no cost. It's a win-win for him. Why did Mark think Eric would leave the company?"

"Eric had been interfacing directly with our investment brokers, only for the business though, not for our personal investments. Ever since the collapse of the financial market, Eric had been pestering Mark to move more heavily into real estate and out of securities. We took a little bit of a beating when the market dropped."

"Everybody did," Tom agreed.

"Mark knew that equities would recover and chose to stay the course. Eric thought that the low values in the real estate market were an opportunity, and he pressured Mark to move funds. '*Solid ground.*'" She smiled at her husband's words. "Eric was impatient. Mark knew that, and assumed Eric would jump at the chance to have a financial stake big enough for him to do his own thing. At the same time we sent you outside the firm for accounting advice, Mark and I locked in a financial management firm to handle the business investments, pension plan, 401K, insurance, that sort of stuff. When we announce the equity ownership arrangement, we'll also announce the restructuring of the financial department. It's just another logical step in our compartmentalizing. The manufacturing facility, the *plant*, is separate from those investments. Mark wanted them to be rock solid. He felt he owed it to the employees. The equity agreement includes a portion of profit that builds as a dividend. Instead of dumping all the net gain over into the financial accounts, it splits growth into two buckets. One bucket is locked up in employee benefits; the other allows the individual to have a little bit of control over their future. They can stay and let it ride, or they can go and not be penalized."

"So," Tom began, "you basically took the money most companies use for executive bonuses, the golden handcuffs, and spread it across your workforce. But you also gave them the key. Anybody with tenure could walk away with their equity at any time, and new employees would start from scratch and build equity along the way. And it's in everybody's best interest for the manufacturing facility to profit."

"Exactly. For Eric, he'd have less responsibility and no change in status, income or equity. Mark assumed he'd leave simply because Eric is so ambitious, and impatient, but it wouldn't matter either way. For Mark, it was a way to diversify and still stick to our core business. He didn't want to get involved in real estate speculation; all Mark ever wanted to do was design. And with the restructuring, the only hole in the organization was a management team to run the plant. Once that's in place, each organization contributes to a symbiotic relationship that supports the whole. With the safeguard that any one function can never sink the ship."

"And Eric would still handle financial responsibilities at the plant?"

"Not directly. Mark intended for Eric's role to be oversight. He would no longer have authority over the whole organization. Eric would be considered Corporate Staff. There would be five departments reporting to Corporate: Engineering; which includes Patents and Licensing; Manufacturing; Contracts; Finance and Human Resources. Eric used to run Finance, which controlled the whole company. With the restructuring, Finance gets downsized to investments only, and then outsourced. Engineering controls licensing, Contracts handles all marketing and proposals, and Manufacturing stands alone as employee owned. Sort of anyway. With the new structure, Eric becomes even more of an executive. Mark was thinking Eric would like the title of CFO, but Mark wasn't naive, he knew Eric enjoyed power more than status. He made it as enticing as he could, but honestly, he wasn't sure what Eric would do."

"Assuming he went rogue on this negotiation thing, what is there to gain?"

"Nothing. That's what makes it so curious. His equity stake isn't inked yet, so he's got nothing to gain from a buyout. And once the paperwork is finalized, he's got nothing to lose either way. I just don't get it," Val shrugged, "something's missing."

"What do you want me to do?" Tom was getting tired. The sun had shifted and was now directly on him, and the hot coffee was causing him to perspire. A light breeze whipped up over the hills and came through the back patio. He lifted his arms slightly and let the breeze dry his shirt. He was glad he'd taken off the jacket.

"Nothing," Val said finishing her coffee. "I want it shut down, but there's nothing he can do officially. If he asks you about it, tell him you gave me the file and I'm considering my options. I'll start setting up meetings for early next week and we can begin the process of communicating these changes. I'm curious where this is coming from, however. If he reaches out to you, try and find out who he's talked to, and how the conversation got started. Also, make it *very* clear that he's not to engage in any negotiation without authorization. At this point, he can still be fired and end up with nothing. There's an ethics clause in his employment agreement. If he's talking to our competitors behind my back I'll fire his ass in a heartbeat. Maintain radio silence unless he brings it up, but if he does, play it however you want; make it sound threatening, or not, I don't care. Just thinking about it pisses me off." She reached across her side of the table and twisted the umbrella putting shade on the two of them.

"Now," she said, leaning on her forearms and addressing her lawyer intently, "let me explain what happened a year ago that prompted all these changes: Mark was following a private company whose work he respected. A totally unforeseen incident disrupted their business. That company no longer exists."

Chapter 6

Robert had spent most of the previous morning disassembling the Triumph, trying to determine what was usable and what should be scrapped. Then he'd spent most of the afternoon aligning a new split exhaust system for a heavily modified Jeep CJ. All the miscellaneous pieces of the exhaust system had been tacked together, and the pipes had been laid to rest on the shop floor awaiting his final welds.

Now it was time to do that thing he was good at: Melting pieces of metal together. Putting all the welds in place was the easy part. A solitary effort behind the tinted glasses, totally focused on pooling and swirling the liquid metal, making sure it went deep enough, but not too deep. For Robert, it was like meditation, but on this particular morning something in the back of his mind kept nagging at him, skirting the edges of his consciousness. He finished the last bead on the exhaust, shut down his equipment, and sat on the shop stool watching the exhaust tubes turn from yellow, to red, to the silver-gray unfinished metal color that deceivingly looked cool enough to touch if you didn't know better. He spun the stool 360 degrees and came back to his view of the exhaust. Then he spun 180 degrees in the opposite direction and stared at the motorcycle frame on the rolling table behind him.

"Hey Joey!" He called toward the back room when the noise of the machines stopped for a minute. "Give me a hand will ya?"

He waited, and just about the time he was ready to call again louder, he heard the slow deliberate sound of one man clapping.

"Very funny!" He yelled. "Are you coming or not?"

"I'm not even breathing hard yet," Joey replied.

"Oh my god, what are you? Twelve? Get in here, I need your help."

Joey showed up at the door, wiping his hands on a shop rag, looking obviously pleased with his little jest.

"What do you need old man?"

"Don't give me that 'old man' crap sonny, your time's a coming, and sooner than you think. Come over here and look at this thing for a minute." Robert walked him to the rear of the Triumph frame and pointed. "Does that look straight to you?"

"Straight? It's mangled! But we're cutting off the whole rear sub frame, right? So, who cares?"

"Yeah. But, no. That's not what I'm talking about. Okay, so the whole rear sub frame is mangled. Most of the damage is on the right-hand side. Caved in like something hit it, or *it* hit something." Robert pointed as he spoke, and they circled the rolling bench together looking at the motorcycle frame. "Now, look at the vertical alignment of the front and rear down-tubes." They both hunkered down, once again at the rear of the frame, eyeballing a horizontal line though the middle, from back to front.

"Okay, yeah, I see what you mean," Joey said. "It's twisted. Will it matter?"

"It'll never track straight."

"Can we fix it?

"Maybe. But it might be easier, maybe even cheaper, just to replace it. I don't want to torch it, and I don't think we have the jigs to press it back into alignment."

"Shit," Joey mumbled, "the cost on this thing keeps creepin' up. I don't want to lose this job."

"Have you talked to our guy yet? Do you know what he wants?"

"No, I'm still researching parts and putting together a couple of designs. The guy's out of town, said he'd come by in a few days."

"Well, just to be safe, add a frame to your parts search. Shouldn't be that hard to find, or too expensive for that matter. But," Robert paused in thought, "the majority of the damage is on the right." Robert pointed, "to my eye, the frame looks twisted to the left?"

"Yeah, I agree," Joey said with a shrug. "So maybe the seat hit a tree on the right side? That would account for all the sub frame damage."

"Okay, I'll give you that," Robert agreed, "but if that's what happened, wouldn't the top be pushed left from center? It looks to me like the bottom has been pushed to the right from center, toward the side of impact."

"What do you make of it Holmes?" Joey said sarcastically, giving Robert his famous 'you're boring me the hell out of me' face.

"Well," Robert began, a little reluctantly, "it looks to me like whoever was riding this bike got hit by a car on the left and thrown into, objects unknown, on the right. Whatever it was, it hit pretty hard to bend that frame. And the rider must have been moving pretty quick for the momentum to cause so much damage on the right."

"Yikes, nasty." Joey said, shaking his head. "That's not a pretty picture at all."

They both turned their attention to the cooled exhaust system, and Joey helped carry it to the back workbench where Robert would begin the process of polishing the tubes to make it look pretty. "Everything's got to look pretty," Robert thought, "even though nobody's ever gonna see it." Well, the customer would see it, once at least. It was a consoling thought.

After lunch, Ken came through the shop to check progress and make some calls. Robert showed him the Triumph frame and explained his observations. Ken was quiet while Robert walked him through what he found. Ken was a good listener. Robert appreciated his attention to detail and respected his opinion. If the frame could be straightened, Ken would know whom to call.

After a few quiet minutes, Ken grabbed a sheet of cold-rolled aluminum scrap and traced a few lines on it. He took it to the back room and sheared the sides to form a polygon that roughly matched the outline of the frame. Together, he and Robert hung a plumb line from the top frame tube and proceeded to shim and clamp the plate onto the frame, first on one side then the other, always maintaining a vertical plane through the center of the fork tube.

"You're right," Ken said finally. He was a man of few words. Then he pointed at the frame and said, "Don't cut that thing up. I need to make a few calls." Robert was optimistic, thinking, "Maybe we can salvage it after all."

Chapter 7

It was an hour and a half past closing time when the police rolled up. Ken was still in his office. Joey had left to go have a beer. And Robert was trying to decide whether to eat, drink, eat *and* drink, or just go to bed when he got home. He'd been working on a small sculpture for the last hour and his neck was beginning to cramp. The sculpture was a three-dimensional rendition of a photo he admired, where a hummingbird in flight was taking a drink from a bright red hibiscus flower. The flower had been easy to make. After cutting the petals from brass sheet stock, he put a wrinkled scallop on the edges, textured the surface by hand, and brazed it together on a wire stem. The hummingbird was the difficult part, and now that it was finished all he had to do was attach the beak to the flower and bend the stem so the whole thing balanced nicely. He was stretching his neck and trying to decide how best to handle the colors. Normally he'd leave his work as bare metal, with heat stresses and natural coloration, but this photo had such vivid reds and greens that he was considering hand painted accents using baked enamel. He spun in his chair when he heard the

cars, and watched as a police cruiser and an unmarked Ford
Crown Victoria stopped just outside the rollup door.

He watched as two uniformed officers, one male and one
female, got out of the cruiser. At about the same time, a man
and a woman also stepped out of the unmarked sedan. The
man exiting from the driver's side was about Robert's age,
maybe a little younger. He wore dark blue slacks, and a lighter
shade, solid blue shirt with a button-down collar. His tie was
maroon, loosened at the neck, and his shoes were soft black
leather with rubber soles. The man had worn his light gray
sport coat in the car and didn't take it off even though the late
afternoon sun wasn't really sport coat weather. His passenger
was a woman, probably ten years younger than her driver,
somewhere around thirty-five, with strawberry blonde straight
hair that just barely touched her shoulders. She was dressed
very professionally. Her shoes matched her blouse and had
low heels. She looked very elegant, and her choice of shoes
seemed comfortable enough for being on your feet all day. The
others were obvious, but this woman didn't look much like a
cop, unless, "maybe," Robert thought, "she was the one in
charge?" The three more obvious police-persons waited while
she opened the back door of the sedan and retrieved a waist
length suit jacket and put it on.

Robert watched as all four casually walked into the shop.
Their eyes roamed the walls and the shop floor until, one by
one, each caught sight of the Triumph frame, where they
locked-on and gravitated toward it like a radar targeting
system. The uniforms were obviously a matched pair, color
coordinated with their car and everything. The other two
looked like the odd couple. The guy in plain clothes looked at
Robert and asked: "Are you the owner?"

Robert pointed toward the office door, and called out
"KEN?"

Ken stepped out of his office and walked their direction with
his hand out like he'd been expecting them all afternoon.
Robert watched as introductions were made all around, then
they approached the stripped down frame with Ken pointing
and explaining all the details that Robert had given him earlier

that day. Nobody looked very happy. The nicely dressed woman kept turning his direction. At one point, Ken motioned toward him saying, "My guy's the one that noticed it earlier this morning." They all turned to look, but only three turned back. The woman kept eye contact for a moment longer, then once again turned her attention to the discussion within the group. As they finished, the cop in the sport coat shook his head and said "Shit, shit, shit. We'll have it all picked up in the morning."

"Hold on," Robert said, coming off the stool and speaking for the first time. "The only evidence of impact is on the frame; the rest of these parts are owned by our customer and he's expecting us to build him a bike. We can't use the frame anyway, take it but leave the rest."

Sport coat didn't look too happy. "This is evidence in a crime," he told Robert with a matter-of-fact air of authority.

"Apparently it wasn't when you auctioned it off to our customer," Robert contested. In his peripheral vision he could see the blonde staring at him. The uniforms looked like they couldn't care less. Ken had raised his hand toward Robert and was about to speak when sport coat beat him to it.

"Up until this morning we had a motorcyclist that dropped his bike in a corner. Now we have a hit and run vehicular manslaughter!"

"Yeah, I get that," Robert said in an amiable tone. His physical systems always fell into an extreme calm when under the most pressure. It helped to disarm negotiations, and gave his mind pinpoint acuity. "But I stripped it all down, god only knows how many people have handled it, there's no extraneous paint, nothing you can match to another vehicle, the only evidence of impact is that frame. And your guys didn't find it because you weren't looking for it." He held his hands up in mock surrender, the universal signal that says '*I don't want to fight with you.*' "Seriously," he continued, "what are you gonna do with it? You're not gonna put a CSI team on it. Your first step is to check out the body shops, and your second step is to revisit the scene of the accident. You know the other vehicle didn't get towed, so it left the scene under its own power." Robert shrugged. "The rest of this bike has way too much damaged from multiple impacts following the initial collision. If you do find the car, assuming it's a car; could be a truck; could be a van; your guys will use CAD software to match the damage, or photos of the damage, assuming it's been fixed already. They'll use a CAD object that describes the original form of the motorcycle compared to the other vehicle. And that's assuming you even get that far. They can't use these parts for anything."

Now he had all their attention, and was beginning to regret having opened his mouth.

"But hey, I don't care, take it if you want, I'm just saying." Sport coat didn't look quite as angry, but Robert still felt the need to back out of the situation.

"Who the hell *are* you?" Sport coat asked. Robert hesitated.

"Are you Robert Jobe?" Asked the blonde, holding out her hand.

"Um. Yes." Robert responded cautiously as he shook the woman's hand. "Do I know you?"

"We've never met," she told him, "but I listened to a presentation you gave at a symposium. In fact, I interviewed at your company."

"I'm sorry to hear that," Robert said jokingly, "but you look smart enough to have turned down the offer."

She tossed her head back and laughed out loud. The sound changed the whole mood in the shop. When she looked at him again, her face turned somber.

"I'm sorry for your loss," she said. Then she turned and walked out to the Crown Vic and got in the passenger seat.

They all watched her walk out. Then they all turned to look at Robert. It made him uncomfortable. He liked being invisible. Now he felt like a flasher that had opened his coat and showed everyone his naked body. He turned, walked to his stool, and sat down with his back to the remaining group. He knew he could wrap himself back up in the coat, but he couldn't make them un-see that part of him he'd just exposed. He was consoled by the knowledge that they'd forget soon enough. They didn't really know him anyway, and there was no reason for them to care about his past.

Sport coat wasn't looking quite so self assured. He turned to Ken and said "I'll give you a call in the morning and let you know what we're gonna do. In the meantime, don't disturb anything." He looked toward Robert, then back to Ken and added: "Please."

Ken shook his hand and assured him that nobody had touched anything since the discovery, and that nobody would until the call came. The customer was out of town and wouldn't be back for a few days, and it was no problem keeping everything at the shop until a decision was made. After walking everyone to the door and watching them drive away, he turned to Robert and asked: "I interviewed at your company?"

Robert took a deep breath and let it out with a sigh, adding, "It's a long story. What's the deal with the cops?"

"That's a long story too," Ken told him, "c'mon, I'll buy you a beer. I'll tell you mine if you tell me yours."

Robert got off the stool and took three steps toward the door. Ken had taken three steps toward his office. They both stopped and looked each other.

"You got beer in there?" Robert asked, pointing toward the little office.

"Yeah, I've got a little mini fridge behind my desk. But don't tell the kid or I'll have to put a lock on it."

"I'm sure as hell not telling Joey, but you'll need to put a lock on it anyway now that you've told me!"

They laughed, and all of a sudden, both men felt like it had been a *very* long day.

Chapter 8

Robert sat on the edge of his bed and tried to stretch. Neck roll, left hand pull on right elbow, right hand pull on left elbow, bend forward, pull up and straighten lower back, stand up, lean against door jamb and bounce on left calf, now the right... ugh. Three beers the previous evening had manifested into a morning headache that made him feel nauseous. There was a time when he could drink all night. Getting old sucked.

The sun had already been up for a couple hours. He never heard the alarm. He'd been jolted awake by a horrible nightmare: Richard Simmons was his physical therapist pushing him through a bouncy aerobic workout. The high pitch voice screaming positive affirmations of joy and laughter, telling him that God would heal his mind, body, soul and spirit, but he needed to "move!" and to "breathe!" and to have "joy in the new day!" Robert wasn't sure if it was the pain in his head causing the nausea or the nightmare.

His common sense told him "Get up, move, normal routine, one foot in front of the other." And so it went: Stretch, aspirin, shower, coffee. But this time there was daylight instead of darkness. Skip the news, no time to stop for breakfast, pick up bagels and more coffee on the walk to work. The bakery was buzzing this morning and as he pushed through the door he heard "Ahrr-Jay!" in a voice that was much too loud and way too happy. His chiropractor had an office in the same little strip mall as the bagel place. "Rafe," Robert nodded at the man as he said his name.

"What a great morning, eh!? I love this weather! You're looking a little rough around the edges! Doing your stretches? Eye-Soh-Metrics baby! Always breathe so you're working on the core too!"

Robert didn't really appreciate his personal medical advice being broadcast to everyone in the bagel shop. The three people in line between them didn't seem to appreciate it either, but the extra attention had no impact on Raphael who was one part chiropractor and one part showman.

"Livin' the dream Rafe, I overdid it on protein shakes last night," Robert told him, the comment grabbing him a few smiles from the other patrons.

Raphael waited by the creamer; Robert finished paying and walked his direction. His chiropractor was a good guy, genuine and sincere. With a big smile he clapped Robert on the shoulder as he put milk in his coffee and said "We were expecting you yesterday. You gonna make it in this week?"

"Probably," Robert said, then with a wry smile added, "I had a dream about you this morning."

"Ho HO!" Raphael said as he walked toward the door. He'd regained his carnival barker voice for the benefit of all who could hear. And everybody could hear. "That sounds like a story I don't need to hear Ahrr-Jay, No-Thank-You. Remember, breathe, core," he said while laughing and patting his perfect six pack abs. "Have faith and do the work and it will all come back to you." The healer pointed at him and winked as he pushed through the door and headed east.

The previous evening had started out easy enough. On their first beer, Ken explained how he thought he had recognized the wrecked motorcycle. A few of his buddies were in a bike club and had introduced him to the man who owned it only one time. No big deal really, but later he'd learned more about the family so it had been in the back of his mind. After he saw the parts, he made some calls and learned that indeed the person he'd met had died in the crash.

Realizing that the rider had been hit by a car and had not simply lost control, he called the police to see if that was how they had the accident listed. As it turned out, no one had looked into it very deeply, and while every road fatality is investigated, there was nothing to indicate another vehicle had been involved. It took most of the day, but after talking to the patrolmen that made the report, they agreed to come take a look. "That was all there was to it really," Ken had said, he just "didn't feel right ignoring something that might be meaningful."

On their second beer, Robert gave him a summary condensed version of his past, explaining that his wife and daughter had died in the car crash that ruined his leg. By the time he was able to get back to work, his small company was pretty much done. But Ken was curious, so Robert told him the history of the company and how they had started with basic support structures for high-tech test equipment at Los Alamos, and eventually developed much more complicated structural designs for the government funded facility.

There were the obvious questions of "why not stay and rebuild" and "why get out" that Robert avoided pretty well, but by the time he was working on his third beer he began volunteering far more information than normal: Robert explained that since the contracts were government funded, he didn't own the designs. When his recovery became a long term proposition, the government shifted procurement volume to second source suppliers. During that time, most of his team spread to the four winds looking for better and more solid opportunities.

He confided that the accident was a freak occurrence. The family had attended a charity dinner and Robert had a few drinks, not too many, but enough so that he asked his wife to drive home. On the way, they hit a patch of black ice and spun over an embankment, rolling a number of times as they careened down the hill. He woke up once in the ambulance while they were working on his leg and they gave him a shot that put him out again. The second time he woke, two weeks had gone by, his head was bandaged and his leg was in a cast. That's when they told him about his family. It took two more operations to get him on his feet. By the time they rolled him out of the hospital there wasn't much left but debt, and questions.

During the time he was in the hospital, small town scuttlebutt had chipped away at his reputation. The police and the insurance company had all the facts, so it wasn't an issue of defending himself against liability. It was an uphill battle against ignorance and conjecture. The questions came from friends, peers, employees, and business contacts. The accident had been given a thirty second spot on the local news channel and all the images were camera shots from a helicopter. The public didn't get the details, only the carnage, so naturally people made up their own versions. The most popular being that Robert was at fault because he was driving impaired.

He'd told his story dozens of times. He'd explained it to his friends and the people who had worked with him for years. But his claim of innocence wasn't being accepted as readily as was the rumor of his being at fault. The elders from his church got together and had a meeting. They sent three of his closest friends to the house for a visit. Robert assumed they were there to provide support, but it turned into an all-night argument. These three men, people that had known him for years, began telling him that he should repent and ask God's forgiveness. They were focused on a cause and effect view of their religion, but they stopped short of using the word "Karma." Robert kept asking "Forgiveness for what?" They couldn't let go of the idea that somehow, he'd been responsible for the events that took his wife and daughter. He endured their logic for as long as he could, believing that their hearts were in the right place. But ultimately, as they hardened their stance, their visit became offensive and he'd kicked them out.

Robert explained to Ken that with his family gone so went his motivation. With everyone he knew questioning his integrity, he felt that the uphill battle to rebuild his reputation in the business community was more effort than it was worth. He had a lot of more important things to deal with than what other people thought of him. He was able to close up shop without claiming bankruptcy, so he packed up what was left and rode off into the sunset, literally, heading west until he hit the Southern California coast.

Discussing it with Ken was both a catharsis and a contagion. It was good to have a friend to talk to, but it made him feel sick all over again. Robert had worked long and hard stuffing all those emotions into a box, wrapping it with chains, and locking it down tight. He'd always been able to keep the lid on, but one more beer and he might have had an even bigger problem: What he didn't share with Ken, what he hadn't shared with anyone, was the visions and the arguments with God he remembered from his time in a coma. Nor did he share the angels that continued to bug him on a daily basis. Nor the headaches. He already knew what people would think about those revelations.

Chapter 9

When Valerie Chase and Tom Lawson entered the small conference room, Rachael McAllister was already waiting for them. Tom was wearing his typical charcoal suit that Rachael considered his "lawyer uniform." Val was dressed smartly in a blue pantsuit with a cream colored top. Rachael was always aware of fashion. She had learned that dressing the part was important, especially in a man's world. Mark had taught her that. He'd helped her climb the ladder of her profession in a way that was merited both on the inside and on the outside. He would never promote her ahead of an accomplishment, but always insisted that she step up her wardrobe a few weeks before he announced a new position for her. For Mark, it was all part of his graduate studies in Organizational Psychology. He was first and foremost an Engineer, but owning his own business forced him to see the bigger picture of outward perception. The glass ceiling offended him, and he was insistent on having good people, and a strong organization needed diversity. But diversity in an organization couldn't survive simply for the sake of diversity. Other companies had tried it and failed. To Mark, the appropriate strategy was to highlight the individual's capability, while gently infusing into the minds of the organization an image that would be accepted. "Acceptance is based on bias," he would say, "and sometimes you have to cater to culture." Another of his aphorisms that Rachael appreciated was "Dinosaurs still roam the earth."

Rachael noted Val's outfit. She was glad to see the shift from basic black, back into the color spectrum. She was also glad that Val had out dressed her. Rachael was well aware of Val's involvement in the business. Mark had confided to her how important and how involved Val was in Chase Industries. For the duration of Rachael's employment, it hadn't looked that way on the outside, with Val acting the part of the socially involved acolyte. Rachael knew that with Mark gone, Val was the *boss*. She wanted very much to support this woman, her respect for Val was palpable, and she owed a lot to Mark Chase.

"Thank you for handling that yesterday Rachael," Val said as they sat, "I wouldn't be able to look at that motorcycle again. It made me ill just thinking about it, I never wanted Mark to buy it, but I never went against his decisions."

Rachael nodded. She kept her face as expressionless as possible out of respect for Val.

"What could they possibly be thinking?" Val was running her fingers through her hair and massaging her scalp. "Mark's gone, what difference does it make?"

Rachael waited a moment to be sure Val was done talking.

"It makes a difference to them," she offered, "if another vehicle was involved they have a bigger problem. The police don't take a hit and run lightly. They're obligated to keep you informed, but you probably won't hear from them until they're finished with their investigation."

"I hope not," Val said, "how did this happen anyway?"

Again, Rachael paused before answering, hoping Val might just let the topic drop. Mark was her mentor and his death was as hard on her as it was on everyone that knew the man. Everyone, that is, with the exception of Val. When she was fairly certain Val expected an answer, she continued.

"The police scrapped out Mark's motorcycle, and somewhere along the way a man handling the salvaged parts noticed a problem. I met the man, his name is Robert Jobe, I interviewed with his company before I took the job here."

Val was staring. Her arm had stopped mid stroke. Her hand was still in her hair.

Tom Lawson turned to Val and asked, "Is that the guy you told me about yesterday?"

It snapped her out of her shock. She straightened her hair and regained her composure.

"I don't know," she told them, coming back into the present and the situation at hand. "But that's not why we're here. I'm sorry I got off on that topic. Rachael," Val stopped and smiled at her employee. "Over the last year Mark and I were making plans to restructure the company. Now that he's gone we have a challenge, a double-edged sword if you will, we need to execute on our plans, but he's not here to supervise them. He and I have tremendous faith in you, and Mark wanted you to take over Engineering."

Rachael was stunned. She blinked a couple of times and made a desperate effort to retain her stoic expression.

"I know it's a lot to take in; you would have reported directly to Mark, but now you'll be reporting to me. I'm going to need your help Rachael, we'll be working this together." Val waited a moment to let it register completely before continuing. "This is what Mark wanted. You know more about our designs than anyone else in the company. Mark made sure of that, which I'm sure, if you think about it, becomes obvious."

She turned to her lawyer who handed her a small batch of papers clipped together. Val removed the clip and thumbed through the stack. When she looked up again, she saw the panic on Rachael's face and held out her hand.

"Relax," she said gently, taking Rachael's hand. "You'll be the head of Engineering. We're separating the company into more discrete departments. Here's how it's going to look." Val slid one set of papers across the table: "Engineering, Manufacturing, Contracts, Finance and HR. You won't be running the whole shooting match like Mark used to do, you'll be working with the heads of these departments as peers and answering to me, as will they. No one person can fill Mark's shoes, but I can't tell you how to do your job the way Mark could either, so in one sense you'll have less responsibility and, in another sense, you'll have more. You're the head of design, and in that capacity, what you say goes. You'll be working most closely with the heads of manufacturing and contracts. Actually, that's not true. You'll be working most closely with me, but your relationship with those two department heads is the key to this management structure."

Rachael was looking the paper over as Val was speaking. Val moved onto the next set of topics without a pause, handing the papers to Rachael one by one.

"Here is the written job description and the salary, here's the breakdown for equity ownership, here's a list of our contract base, and here's the restructured benefits package. Now, I need to ask a personal favor from you." She reached across the table and gathered all the paperwork she'd just handed Rachael. Taking them back, she arranged them neatly on the table and put the clip back into place.

Rachael was still slightly in a state of shock. "Of course, anything you need." She said after composing herself.

"We haven't made any announcement yet, so what I'd like for you to do is, without speaking to anyone along the way, take these directly to your car, drive home, read through them, and then bring them to me at the house this afternoon so we can discuss it further. Will you do that for me?"

"Yes Mrs. Chase. I can do that. Thank you." Rachael was nodding her head. Val held the clipped stack of papers out to her, but when Rachael reached for them Val didn't let go. When Rachael looked up, Val held her questioning gaze and said, "And Rachael; from now on it's Val."

Rachael McAllister went to her office and retrieved her purse. Without stopping or commenting to anyone, she walked straight through the parking lot and found her car. Feeling a little dazed, she unlocked the door and got settled behind the wheel. The door closed with a satisfyingly solid thump, sealing out the noise, leaving her quietly suspended in her emotions. She grabbed the wheel with white knuckles, took a deep breath, and cried for a full ten minutes.

When Rachael had left, Tom turned to Val and said, "That felt weird." Val returned his look and said with a smile, "You ain't seen nothin' yet." She picked up the phone and asked her admin to bring Eric Pierce to the conference room.

"Why ask her to the house?" Tom asked.

"There are a few things I want to discuss with her, that's all. I want her to relax. She can't do that here."

There were two quick knocks at the door before it opened and Eric's head poked through the gap.

"Val," he said affectionately, "it's so good to see you."

"It's good to see you too Eric," Val said as she shook his hand. "Please close the door and have a seat."

When he was settled, she smiled across the table at him and said, "Now, what's all this nonsense about a buy out?"

To Tom, Eric's expression looked like he'd just taken an icepick to the forehead.

"Uhm... it... it was just something on the table that I thought you should know about."

"How did it get on the table?" Val was looking straight at him, but Eric had broken her gaze and his eyes were bouncing around the room while he tried to gather his thoughts.

"How did it get on the table?" he repeated. "Well, let me think. At the last conference Mark and I attended, we were approached with the idea. It was just an option that I felt should be considered. Something you should know about, now that Mark's gone."

Val didn't respond. Eric started to fidget a bit less, thinking he'd made a good recovery and might now be back on solid ground. Val let the silence become uncomfortable. When it looked like Eric was going to start in again, Val took the lead.

"Right. Okay. That would be the same conference where Mark entered into a handshake agreement with our prime. You know, the competitor of the folks that want to buy us out. Is that right?"

The ground moved under Eric's feet again. "Uhm... I'm not sure. It could be. Yeah, I guess that's probably right."

"Well thank you for bringing it to my attention Eric. I've given it my consideration and the answer is no. And, if Tom hasn't told you, you are legally obligated to not speak of it again to anyone. Now that we're on contract, if these people call you, both Tom and I will need to know about it immediately. This is our first government contract Eric. Federal law is at play here, it's not business as usual. You understand what I'm telling you right?"

"Yes, of course," Eric said.

Tom chimed in: "There's information disclosures, Defense Contract Audit Agency oversight, ethics considerations. There are a LOT of considerations and we need to be very sensitive not step over the line contractually. We can't have ANY contact with them unless we report it through channels."

"I understand," Eric reassured them.

"Good," Val said. "Have you had ANY contact with these people, email or otherwise, prior to today?"

"Uhm… no, of course not." Eric replied, again breaking eye contact.

She held her hand out and Tom placed another clipped stack of papers in them like a nurse hands a scalpel to a surgeon. "Mark was very fond of you," she began; the intentional act of not including herself in that comment was completely lost on Eric. "As you know, he was in the process of reorganizing the company. Effective immediately, this is your new position and your new responsibilities." She slid a selection of the papers across the table for him to review. "As you can see, you make more money and have less to worry about. Mark knew you'd be pleased with the arrangement." She had learned from her husband to pre-sell change when dealing with people. "Now, Mark wanted to make sure you had options." She paused for effect. "He knew how ambitious you are and he didn't want to hold you back. So, as a legacy employee, here is the equity agreement that's been put in place. When you read it, you'll see that your shares are guaranteed. What that means is that you can stay and help build the company, or you can choose to leave and it won't have a negative impact on you financially."

She stood indicating that the meeting was over and held her hand out to their now ex-finance manager. "Take your time making a decision Eric, but I need to know what you wish to do by Monday. We intend to make announcements next week. Don't feel obligated by loyalty. Mark is showing his loyalty to you right there in black and white, and he would want you to do whatever you feel makes the most sense for your future."

Eric Pierce realized he was standing. His eyes were still on the paper in his hand. It had been a reflex action that occurred when Valerie stood, he hadn't consciously willed his legs to perform. As his senses came back to him, he closed his mouth and quickly shook Val's hand. "Thank you, Valerie," was all he could think to say. As he walked to the door he heard Tom tell him, "Please don't mention this to anyone until after the announcements are made next week." He turned and nodded telling them he understood. He walked back to his office in somewhat of a daze, the colors of his familiar environment taking on a surrealistic hue. Walking into that meeting, he had naively believed that the grieving widow was going to ask him to take control of the company.

"You're right," Tom said, "this day is getting curiouser and curiouser. What do you think he's going to do?"

"He'll leave," Val said with confidence. "He's crushed. I really don't know what he expected. Did he seriously believe I would sell my company? Oh, and by the way, he was lying about not having contact. I want the email system reviewed. If there's any evidence of improper communication it will need to be disclosed.

"You know Tom, Eric worked with Mark on the restructuring, but he wasn't privy to all the details. He couldn't possibly have thought he could fill Mark's shoes, but who knows? He never struck me as very bright, but I didn't think he was *that* dumb. Mark always felt Eric was, well, the word he used was *'entertaining.'*"

"What now?" Tom asked her.

"Our work here is done for the day. HR and Contracts are already in place. All I have to think about now is the plant. The next few days will be interesting though," she said, smiling at Tom. "Rachael won't say anything, but I can't say the same for Eric. It will be very interesting to hear what information gets circulated throughout the rumor mill."

Chapter 10

Having immersed himself in work, Robert was feeling a bit closer to normal by early afternoon. The headache was gone and his muscles had loosened. Having skipped taking time off for lunch, he used the time to put some finishing touches on a few jobs, polishing parts that weren't obvious to the casual observer, pushing their cosmetic look beyond what the customer expected. It really didn't take much extra effort to do a superior job, and Ken's customers always appreciated the unexpected attention to detail. Word of mouth business was growing nicely, along with their reputation.

Now, as he was completing his last task for the day, he was thinking about food. If he didn't eat soon, he'd be dealing with a different type of headache. He pulled a protein bar from his toolbox and was munching on it while wiping residual grit off the recently buffed metal ring that surrounded the locking mechanism on a custom wrought iron gate. If he was careful with his blood sugar level, he could make it through late afternoon and then grab an early dinner. That plan would give him three or four hours he could devote to colorizing the hummingbird. His mind had drifted back to paint selection and curing techniques when he heard Ken calling his name.

"You've got a phone call," Ken told him.

Robert was a little taken aback. "From who?" he asked. He didn't know anyone that would call him, and those few people he did know, wouldn't know where he worked. Ken just waved him over and disappeared back into the office.

When Robert walked in, the phone was off the cradle sitting on Ken's desk. He pointed at it. Robert picked it up and tentatively said "hello?"

"Mr. Jobe, this is Rachael McAllister, we met yesterday?"

"Yes, of course. What can I do for you Ms. McAllister?"

"My employer owned the motorcycle we were examining yesterday. His wife would like to meet with you. Would that be possible?"

Robert was quickly running different excuses through his mind, fully intending to graciously decline when he saw Ken nodding his head to the affirmative and giving him an enthusiastic thumbs up.

"I suppose that would be possible," he heard his voice say while he gave Ken a shrug and a questioning look, "can I ask what this is about?"

"Thank you Mr. Jobe, we would greatly appreciate that. I'd much rather she explains the situation to you herself if you don't mind. Can you come say, around six this evening? We're not that far from you."

He wrote the address and a few directional notes on a scratch pad Ken had pushed his direction and said his goodbyes.

"What the hell was that about?" Robert asked when he hung up the phone.

"I'm not sure, but whatever that woman wants is fine with me. She and her husband are major contributors to the cancer treatment center we've got Danny in, so whatever she needs, tell her I'm willing to help."

"She wants to meet with me at six. I suppose I should take off and grab a shower."

"Do it," Ken told him.

Robert had to dig deep to find an appropriate outfit. He had kept only one of his old suits, and to his dismay, moths had eaten a hole in the slacks. He had one pair of casual dress pants that he matched with a long sleeved, cream colored dress shirt. Outside of that combination all he had were jeans and a pair of swim trunks. His shoes were quite scuffed, but at least they were black leather, much like the cop's shoes yesterday. As he looked in the mirror, first he tried the shirt normally, then rolled the sleeves halfway up, then decided against it and put them back down. He shrugged on the suit jacket thinking it might serve as a sport coat, but the combination just didn't work. On the way out, he grabbed his windbreaker in the event their meeting lasted longer than he was hoping.

Not having a pass for the toll road, he pulled out onto Highway 1, then south past Jamboree to Newport Drive. The old truck hadn't been driven much since he'd come west to work for Ken. It shook out the kinks and got its juices flowing on a short stretch of the freeway. Checking his notes, Robert found the street, then the address. Pulling into the circular drive was impressive. Parking behind a late model BMW sitting next to a Land Rover was humbling. It was a Mediterranean style house, subtle and in no way opulent, but very stylish. The neighborhood was well manicured and he could tell the view from any of these homes would add half a million dollars to the property value.

Valerie Chase answered the door dressed in a pair of white slacks and a yellow blouse. Robert thought her attractive, in a regal sense, her mostly plain features highlighted by her choice of style. She was elegant, yet casual, good handshake and eye contact; she spoke with confidence and moved with grace.

"Mr. Jobe, thank you for coming."

"Mrs. Chase," he said taking her hand. After stepping into the foyer, he added, "I'm sorry for your loss" as she closed the door behind him.

"Yes. Thank you. Please come in," she replied, leading him to the right, around the stairs and into the living room. Rachael McAllister was sitting on the patio just off the open French doors that provided a visual separation between the formal living room and the moderate dining table. She rose and stepped to the door as they came into the room.

"Good to see you again Mr. Jobe," Rachael said, greeting him with a handshake.

"Please call me Robert."

"I will, thank you, please call me Rachael."

"Would you like a drink?" Val asked, as she turned toward the small bar along the corner wall of the dining area adjacent to the kitchen.

"Maybe a gin and tonic, if you have it."

Val retrieved a highball glass from the cabinet and placed it on the bar next to a bottle of Canada Dry.

"If you don't mind, I'll let you mix it yourself," Val told him, "the ice is in the door of the fridge."

Robert appreciated the casual approach. He checked the setting on the fridge, then dropped three of the half-moon shapes of frozen water into his glass. He splashed an inch of Bombay onto the ice then filled it about three quarters full with tonic and gave the glass a little swirl to mix the liquids.

"I'm sorry we don't have any fresh limes," Val said as he turned toward them. "Things have been a little hectic lately. I've not done any formal entertaining for months."

"This is just fine, Mrs. Chase. Really," he added with a smile and a nod, "it's exactly the way I would make it at home." The indirect light coming from the patio bounced off the walls of the dining area softening her facial features. It enhanced the lines of fatigue around her eyes. The visual impact was that she had aged three years during the walk from the entryway to the dining area. "Understandable," Robert thought, "given her circumstances."

"If you don't mind, I'd like to sit on the patio. And please call me Val, may I call you Robert?" She turned and led them outside. They settled in, adjusting their seating arrangement to maximize the view and avoid direct sunlight. "I find myself sitting out here a lot," Val said with a deep breath. "Looking to the horizon and trying to imagine what my future will hold."

Robert was searching his mind for something to say. All he knew of this woman, and her situation, was that she'd recently lost her husband. He still had no idea why she'd invited him here, or how Rachael was involved. He was relieved when she continued, breaking the silence before it turned awkward.

"Let me explain why I asked you here today," she began. "Rachael told me she'd met you yesterday. The police called and I wasn't able to deal with the situation, Rachael was gracious enough to go downtown and meet with them on my behalf." She turned to make eye contact and said, "My husband was familiar with your work. I'm familiar with your situation only on a cursory level, but I would like to also extend the sentiment of 'I'm sorry for your loss.'" She turned again toward the horizon. "It's funny," she continued, "people don't know what to say. They take your hand and stare into your face. Some exude anguish. Others try to be uplifting, some get religious." She took a sip of her drink. "At one point, I swore to myself I was going to punch the very next person that tried to tell me Mark was 'in a better place now' or that 'God has called him home'. Every time I heard 'it was his time' I thought to myself 'no it wasn't'. If people said 'it was God's will' I wanted to scream: 'Then God made a mistake!'" She scoffed and took another sip. "There's really nothing they *can* say is there? Some of my friends have simply avoided me while others won't leave me alone. I suppose there's no appropriate sentiment. I'm sorry for your loss is about as courteous as you can get. When people try to say more, they usually end up tripping over their own tongue."

Robert sat in silence. He wasn't sure where she was headed with the conversation. Everything she said was true, and for her it was still new and very raw. All his old feelings of shock and disbelief were coming back to him and he envisioned himself sitting on that old strongbox where he kept his emotions, making sure the lid stayed closed tight.

"But that's not why I asked you here either, I'm sorry for delaying. We all have to move forward and the situation's different for everyone at times like this, I'm just not quite sure how to get started."

"I'm sorry to admit I'm not familiar with your husband or his work," Robert volunteered. "And I'm not sure how he knew about me. Maybe you can start by telling me how I can help you? Feel free to just say it, I promise I won't be offended, no matter how it sounds."

"There's no reason why you should be familiar with Chase Industries," Val continued. Robert let her build up to it, whatever *it* was. "Our contracts are all commercial, and our designs are held privately. Mark stayed very active within the industry, going to symposiums and conferences, reading papers and listening to presentations. He never shared much; it was all a matter of gathering information and fact finding, keeping his finger on the pulse of technology. You were one of the few people he kept track of, as far as that goes, whenever he saw your name associated with a presentation he made sure to read it."

"Government contracts," Robert told her, "publish or perish. That was my primary marketing path. Whenever I created something I was proud of, the only way to get the word around was to submit a paper. The government owned all my designs; we would get exclusive manufacturing rights for a couple years. After that, they put proposals out for competitive bids. If we could innovate, we would win the follow-on contracts."

"We never bid on any government contracts until recently," Val said, "and even now, we bid only as a subcontractor where the prime is licensing our design. At least until they find a way to copy it I suppose." She took another sip of her drink. "When Mark heard about your situation, it opened his eyes to the risks we faced in our own company. He and I built this company our whole lives. Twenty-five years of marriage, twenty-two years working together, building a life, a legacy. Mark realized that if anything happened to him..." She shook her head. "He wanted to mitigate that risk. A year ago, we started restructuring the company to do just that: Mitigate the risk. And now he's gone. Everything can change in the blink of an eye."

"It sounds to me like your husband was a very astute businessman Val."

She turned to make eye contact again. "The company is in a very good place. I feel guilty saying this, but we've benefitted greatly from your misfortune. I wanted to meet you. I wanted to thank you. And I wanted a chance for us to chat before I decided. I'd like to ask for your help."

Robert felt the urge to run, but he didn't know which way to go. She saw the panic in his face, but he knew she couldn't read it; she had no idea the roller coaster ride his emotions were taking. He calmed himself and tried not to change expressions. He didn't even know what kind of help she was hoping for, but instinct told him to get the hell out now! A little voice in the back of his head was screaming *coward,* while another was telling the first to *fuck off!* He took a breath and drank a little of his gin and tonic. He heard Ken telling him "...whatever that woman wants is fine with me."

Thinking he might have found a tactful way to avoid the situation and let her down gently, he told her "You said it best Val: 'We all have to move forward and the situation's different for everyone'. I'm still trying to figure out what that looks like for me, but I've decided it should look different than before. I can't continue in this industry, and I'm not sure how I can help you. Besides, your husband seems to have already handled the circumstances that caused me to fail. He was a much better businessman than I ever was, or ever could be. Your business is much bigger than mine. I don't think I can be much help."

She was ready for him. "Mark always said you learn more from your failures than your successes. He was a big believer that experience was the best teacher." She smiled at Robert. "He was quick to add that it was more cost effective when it's someone else's experience."

"I don't want to go back to work in the industry," Robert said gently but firmly.

"Then I won't offer you a job," she told him, "but I would like to have you as an advisor on a limited basis. We should be able to make it through our transition in a matter of weeks. You'll be working very closely with Rachael, that's why I've asked her to this meeting. I'm happy to pay you as a consultant."

"It's not the money," he told her.

"Good" she said.

"Damn!" he thought. "Maybe I could have priced myself out of the market." All the while he was mulling it over; Ken's words kept being repeated over and over in his subconscious. He looked across the table at Rachael. "How do you feel about this?"

"I'll take all the help I can get," she told him.

"You're not just saying that because the boss is sitting next to you?"

"I always speak my mind. Mark appreciated it, and I believe, so does Val. I'm committed to this company. If I didn't want you here, I don't think Val would have invited you. But that's just my intuition speaking, I would never be so arrogant as to oppose anything the Chase's suggest. They've always asked for my opinion, and I've always been honest. If she directed me to work with you, I would do my job no matter what I thought about it, but that's not what this is."

Robert nodded. "Okay," he said finally, "I suppose I'll need to get some decent clothes. This is all I've got other than jeans. How can I help?"

"Expense whatever you need," Val said, "and keep track of your hours. My lawyer will set up a standard contract with non-disclosure agreements for you to sign in the morning. There are two specific areas where we want you to consult: Our restructuring plans are being executed and the transition is already underway. We've accounted for those things we *think* we know, but you've experienced the worst, and we don't know what we *don't* know. I want your opinion regarding any holes you see in our plan."

"And the second thing?"

"I have to select someone to lead our manufacturing facility. Naturally there are a number of qualified candidates. Rachael is a designer, and my background is business management. You, like Mark, handled design and production. After you get a clear picture how the plant is structured, and the type of production we do, you'll have a better understanding of our strengths and weaknesses. We'd like your help in the interviewing process, I want to be sure we're choosing the right person to guide us forward." She made it clear the decision was all hers, but nodded toward Rachael whenever she used the inclusive "we".

Robert nodded his agreement.

"Good! I'm glad that's settled. Welcome aboard. Would you like me to contact your employer?"

"That's not necessary," Robert told her. "My boss's son is receiving chemo treatments at the children's hospital. He recognized your name. If it weren't for him, I wouldn't be at this meeting. To quote his words, 'whatever she needs, tell her I'm willing to help.'"

He saw the change in her expression. He couldn't read it, but he knew that his comment had sent her emotions on a roller coaster ride of their own. She composed herself quickly.

"Alright then, please thank him for me. If you have plans we'll see you to the door, but Rachael has graciously accepted my dinner invitation and I'm famished. If you'd care to join us we can continue this discussion at the restaurant."

Chapter 11

Eric Pierce sat on a low backed stool and rattled the ice in his empty glass saying to the bartender, "I need another one of these Marty." He held the glass up in his right hand, in his left were the papers he'd brought from work, and he was rereading them for the third time. He still couldn't believe what had happened. He'd returned to his desk and read everything through the first time. Then, just before lunch, he packed his briefcase and walked out. He'd driven straight to his girlfriend's bar and read the agreement a second time over his first scotch and soda. And now, after having some single digit number of drinks that he couldn't quite remember exactly, which he thought was strange since he'd always been pretty good with numbers, he still couldn't quite believe it. Had he read the situation wrong? As he waited for another dose of pain reliever it occurred to him that more likely than not it was Val who had stepped in and changed the rules.

No bartender came. When he looked up, the owner of the bar was standing in front of him. She was tall and muscular. At six foot, she was taller than Eric by almost three inches, which wouldn't be so bad if she didn't always insist on wearing four-inch heels, which made her tower over him when they were out together. With broad shoulders, an athletically toned body, olive skin and long straight black hair, she was striking, and he enjoyed being seen with her. She was dressed in her typical attire for the bar: Tight black tank top and black jeans that looked like she had to lie down to get them on. And of course, there were the heels. She was proud of her body, and her height, which gave her a feeling of power. Owning a bar was a tough business and she'd fared well, but only after proving multiple times that she was tough enough to tough it out with the toughest of them. And now, they finally gave her the respect she always knew she deserved.

"Starting a bit early aren't you lover? You know how it affects your performance. Are you gonna get drunk every night this week?"

Eric looked around self-consciously, he didn't always like the way she treated him.

"I'm just having a rough day. I didn't expect you back from the gym so early."

"You should try it once in a while, it would do you good. What's with the papers?"

He put them away. He was almost afraid to tell her, but he was going have to discuss it with her eventually. After a few moments he decided now was as good a time as any, and the scotch had boosted his courage.

"I need to talk to you. Fix us a drink and let's get a booth."

When they were settled, Eric scanned the bar to make sure their conversation was at least semi private.

"I think we're screwed," he told her. "The restructuring cut off my signature authority. Those papers? That's my new job description. I think she expects them to be my walking papers.

"What do you mean we're screwed? You told me you were gonna end up running the place?" She was obviously angry. This new wrinkle was not part of her plan, and Eric's scheme was only a small part of *her* plan. It always made her angry when he talked like some great strategist.

It made Eric very uncomfortable when she got angry and he

scanned the bar again out of nervous habit.

"I've been pushed aside. I have less authority, not more."

"Aren't you still their chief financial guy?"

"Well, yeah." He didn't explain to her that his new position only gave him oversight and not operational authority. He didn't dare confide in her the fact that the investment accounts were now completely out of reach.

"THEN FIX IT!"

He scanned the bar again.

"STOP looking around. I want to know how you're gonna fix this."

He fidgeted with his glass and wouldn't make eye contact. He hated it when she got like this.

"Look," he began, "I've got equity. I can leave and cash out, but it's not enough. If you put something in, it *would* be enough!"

"There it is," he thought, "I've TOLD her. Take THAT bitch! I'm drawing the line, it's time for you to step up."

She watched him squirm across the table from her. In the silence, his face went from afraid, to angry, to apprehensive, to questioning. She could read him like a book.

"Now you listen to me," she began, trying to decide exactly how to play the hand, "that was not our deal. I told you up front I'm not putting up this bar on your big idea. This bar is my retirement plan; you're the one that said we had a brass ring at the tips of our fingers. You made promises to me. I expect you to keep them."

"I'm thinking about my retirement too, ya know? If I cash out, everything I've got is on the line. I'm thinking maybe we should just let our options expire. Maybe it's best in the long run if I just stay with the company."

"That's bullshit! You lied to me you spineless bastard! You can't stay with the company anyway. Eventually they'll do an audit and find out what you did, and then you'll lose that precious retirement for sure! No, you're all in, and you need to figure this out."

"What are you so upset about? You've got *nothing* at stake."

"I've got more at stake than you know." She stood and

picked up his half-finished drink. "Now get the fuck outa my bar. You're not coming over tonight either, I don't want to have anything to do with you right now."

"Dabs," he said as she turned away.

"And don't call me until you've got a plan. You're gonna fix this, so help me…" She left off God.

"Dabs!" He said again as she walked away from their booth. "I had a plan, but it fell through! DABS!"

She walked straight past the bar and into the back office. Eric thought about going after her, but after a moment of reflection he decided it would be best for him to leave.

On the way to his car, he wondered how he was going to "fix it" as she put it. She made it sound so simple: "Fix it." Easy for her to say, she didn't know one thing about his business, all she did was run a lousy bar. He was angry that she would put it all on him. They were partners, they were supposed to work together, and this wasn't how you treated your partner. She was being pissy and he didn't like it. "I could have done this deal without you bitch," was what he thought. He stopped in his tracks. Did he say that out loud? Looking around, he was relieved to see it didn't matter; he was alone in the parking lot. "No, that's not right either," he acknowledged. He couldn't have put the deal together without her, but it was starting to get complicated, and he was beginning to question the wisdom of his partnership. What did she mean with "I've got more at stake than you know?" "She's got nothing at stake," he thought, "that was just another way to manipulate me."

Why were women always trying to manipulate him? Mark trusted him, why couldn't Val? It was a clear choice for him to take over, and now she'd cut him off from the financial accounts, *and* pushed him out of both contracts and manufacturing. His plan would have made everybody money, why couldn't Mark see that? As he sat in the car, his mind raced. He was not going to give Val Chase the satisfaction of watching him walk away, and he was not going to give up his safety net if Dabs wasn't willing to give up hers. But most importantly, he was not going to let the deal fall through, if only to prove to Dabs that when push came to shove, he could handle it without her help. He opened the car door and began to step out, then realized he hadn't driven anywhere yet. He slammed it closed. She kicked him out of the bar? What a BITCH! He wasn't done drinking.

Putting the car into gear, he carefully maneuvered onto the road and unconsciously headed toward the beach. "The bars are nicer down there anyway. Maybe she'll calm down in a few hours," he thought to himself. He decided to have a bite to eat and a couple more drinks, then give her a call and see if she'd changed her mind. "Maybe, if she calms down a bit," he thought with mild hope and anticipation, "I can still go by her place tonight." But he knew that either way he had to come up with a new plan.

Chapter 12

When the alarm sounded, Robert followed his normal morning routine. It had been a fitful night. He'd woken to check the clock multiple times, but didn't feel nearly as tired as he was expecting. He dreamt about the Chase family. He respected how Val and her husband Mark had done so much to protect what they built, something Robert had failed to do when he had the opportunity. And yet, Mark was taken "in the blink of an eye" as Val had said. It didn't seem fair, and fairness was the pervading concept throughout last night's dreams.

At one point, the Archangel of Justice appeared with fiery hair, assuring him that all would be put into divine order. The vision actually made him sad and depressed. The realization that he was not truly mourning the loss of his family, but rather just feeling sorry for himself, came in the form of Uriel, the Fire of God, sending him a warning. Robert kept waking and dozing, checking his alarm to see the time, worried that he'd slept late. Every time he turned to the clock in fear, he'd roll back into bed and wonder why the feeling of panic? He'd listened carefully to make sure he hadn't heard some foreign sound while he slept. Then as he dozed off again, he'd start feeling guilty about his own self-centered grief and wham! He'd be jolted awake with the word rolling around his head like 'it's not what you think,' and 'it's not how it looks,' and finally 'be careful of the role you play.'

It was this last thought that woke him for good and left him in confusion. Thinking back on all the times he awoke during the night, he wondered about the lingering question: The why? What was the message? He hadn't overslept, it wasn't his self-pity, it wasn't a thump in the night. And it wasn't Uriel arguing with Raguel. It was specifically for him, but the meaning was obscured. "Typical," he thought as he stood under the hot water, "tell me something else I don't understand." Valerie Chase's situation was too similar to his own experience, causing him trouble in differentiating the message. Yet somehow, everything about the Chase situation was different from his own, so why the confusion?

Today he had to drive rather than walk. Robert's first stop was the fab shop where he explained to Ken what he'd been asked to do, and how long he thought it would take. Ken reassured him that they'd be all right for the next few weeks and encouraged Robert's support for Valerie Chase. While they were chatting, Detective Sport-coat showed up with a van and a uniformed officer.

The police picked up the motorcycle frame and a few of the broken pieces; informing Ken he could keep the leftover parts. As Ken began to volunteer information regarding the family's request for help, the detective's curiosity was piqued.

"Help with what exactly?" He asked defensively.

"With business matters," Robert told him, "nothing to do with the accident."

The detective stared at him expressionless, apparently waiting for more information. Robert grew uncomfortable in the silence and began to respect the tactic even more as he volunteered additional information. It was like he couldn't help himself, but as he spoke he heard the warning: Be careful of the role you play.

"Look," he said, "I had a death in the family, and the result was, I lost my business. Mrs. Chase knew my background and asked if I could help verify that they haven't left themselves open to unknown risk."

"Mrs. Chase's net worth is not at risk, she stands to gain millions from the life insurance alone. How long have you known Mrs. Chase?" Sport-coat quizzed.

"We met yesterday for the first time."

More stoic silence ensued until Robert got irritated.

"Call her! Call the blonde you met yesterday! Ken will tell you, I didn't even want to take the job, he practically insisted!" Robert calmed down for a minute and added. "Besides, *I'm* the one that got *you* involved remember? You guys had already closed this case!"

That seemed to snap Sport-coat back into line. The logic was fairly irrefutable.

"Just doing my job," he said without apology, handing them each a business card. "If there's anything you guys think of, or anything Mrs. Chase says, or anybody else you run into; if anything, even remotely pops up, feel free to give me a call. We got nothing at the body shops. It's turned into a routine hit and run. We're probably not gonna find the guy unless we get lucky and he's driving around with a busted headlight. Maybe a patrolman will stop him and think twice before writing a ticket and letting him go."

Robert glanced at the business card and said, "Earnest Derrota... Sincere Defeat?"

The detective glared at him. "I prefer Serious Beating. I get teased more at family get-togethers and holidays than I do downtown. Most of the gringos don't get the reference." He turned to Ken and said, "You can call me Ernie." He turned back toward Robert and said, "You, smart ass, can call me Detective Derrota." They shook hands and watched him go.

The next stop for Robert was a men's store where he picked up a decent off the rack suit, an additional jacket and pair of slacks, four shirts and two ties. The combination gave him four outfits, and if he were clever with his mixing and matching he wouldn't get caught out wearing the same outfit twice in one week. That is of course, provided there were plenty of introductions and he didn't find himself working with the same faces every day. He figured it would take a few days to settle in, and if it looked like he'd be working with a small team, he could always buy a couple more shirts and ties. If he were lucky, the jackets would spend most of their time on a chair or draped across his arm, allowing him to extend his wardrobe further simply by wearing them. The salesman kept pushing shoes, but Robert knew he'd be unable to last the day in patent leather.

After finding a pair of soft-soled shoes, Robert's final stop for the day was the Chase offices, where he met with Tom Lawson to sign his contractor agreement and non-disclosure agreement. Tom walked him around, showing him to the conference room that had been reserved for introductory meetings scheduled for the following morning. He did not see Val or Rachael. Tom led him to an empty office and introduced Robert to the admin for the area. After waiting around forty minutes, the IT guy finally showed up and set up Robert's account and left him with a laptop to use that could log in remotely to the company servers.

Leaning back in his chair, he surveyed his little makeshift office. He looked out the window into the Chase parking lot. The comfort of familiarity came back to him. It wasn't like the new technology companies, where creature comforts and freedom were expected to foster employee creativity; it was more like the old days. The dull gray and olive drab metal desks that were so often the motif of old government contractors had been replaced with new modular furniture, but the feeling of an engineering firm was the same: A good idea, and lots and lots of paper. Computer files had now replaced the majority of the paper, but he was familiar with that scenario also, having grown up in the industry while it made the transition.

The company revolved around Product Data Management systems, Production Planning software, and gads of information management applications that allowed for notes, ideas, and lessons-learned to all be captured and shared online.

He could do this. Maybe one step back would allow him to take two steps forward. Robert was actually looking forward to the challenge. The thought made him uneasy, but he didn't know why exactly.

Chapter 13

The phone rattled the top shelf of her locker and when she checked, it showed that Eric had called three times. She clicked it off and put it back. After an hour and a half of kicking and punching the bag at the Muay Thai studio, she'd been able to release the anger she felt earlier in the bar. She liked the martial arts instructor here, a lot, and wondered if she'd made a mistake hooking up with Eric. He wasn't really her type but after months of him hitting on her she'd had a drink with the man wondering if a change of type might not be a bad idea.

Her type in the past had always been hot heads that thought they could smack her around. They thought that, at least, until they tried the first time and found out different. She was raised by her father and his brother. Being Scots-Irish, fighting was second nature to them, but they treated her with respect and gave her a lot of space. Maybe too much space for a little girl, even though she liked the freedom and solitude they provided. At fourteen she'd gone to a party that got out of hand. A twenty year old had drank too much beer and started to grope her. When she fought back, he pushed her down and she hit her face on an armchair. By the time Dabs got home the bruise had swelled to the size of a fist.

Walking in the door, her father and uncle immediately questioned her, and fearing reprimand she told them the story bit by bit. When the picture became clearer to the two men, they packed Dabs in the car without any punishment or harsh words. They drove her back to the party and reassuringly walked her inside. She could still feel their large hands gently resting on her shoulder, providing comfort and safety. Once they had successfully identified the young man that had trespassed on the little girl, they promptly beat him within inches of his life while she watched in horror. A few other party goers had tried to object, but they too left the party in search of medical help.

The incident made a lasting impression on the teenager and it didn't help her reputation at school or in the neighborhood. The girls tended to shun her and the boys were simply afraid. She had a hot temper like her father and uncle. Living with men, she grew up in a physical environment and excelled in sports and ultimately fighting. Her mother had named her Dabria. According to her father, the name meant "the name of an angel" in her mother's Latin-American culture. Dabs had endured some grade school chiding for her unusual name and she often resolved those disputes with her fists. Once, while sitting in detention for pummeling three boys on the school playground, she looked her name up on the internet and read that it meant "Angel of death". Dabs decided she liked that translation better than her mother's and began wearing black to increase the intimidation factor.

As she matured, Dabs grew into her mother's features and her father's muscular build. She was tall and lean, with olive skin and long black shiny hair. At seventeen she was catching the eye of men twice her age, but still intimidating her fellow high schoolers. At nineteen, she married a man in his early thirties and helped him set up their bar, waitressing in the evenings even though she was under age. It was a tempestuous marriage and a physical relationship, but a lucrative business, especially when her husband started selling cocaine on the side. Dabs enjoyed the conflict, feeling like she could hold her own with any man, but at her core she was still just a kid.

It was two years into the marriage, when late one night things got out of control. At nearly closing time Dabs walked into the storage room and found her husband, stoned half out of his mind, and a fellow waitress enjoying her break a little too intimately. She grabbed the woman by the hair and dragged her out the back door, threw her to the ground and told her she was fired. When her husband objected, Dabs promptly kicked over his Harley. The man belted her, knocking Dabs unconscious. When she awoke, she was lying on the sofa in their apartment with an ice pack on her face. Her husband was asleep in the adjacent armchair. Dabs stood, walked to their garage, retrieved a two-foot long section of pipe, returned to the house and extracted her revenge.

By the time the police arrived, Dabs' husband had a broken leg, two broken arms, numerous contusions plus broken ribs and a concussion. They were both arrested, but her black eye gave plausibility to a claim of self-defense. In the subsequent divorce, Dabs' husband was granted a restraining order and payment for all medical bills. Dabs got the bar.

Her relationships over the next ten years were better, if only for that fact that her sex life was now completely under her control. The bar had done well, it turned out she had a natural talent for the business, and it provided a constantly moving stream of patrons from which to pick and choose bed partners. She had little tolerance for weakness and even less for aggression. Guys would hit on her, which she enjoyed. Flirting back became a sport, the object being to find a man with enough backbone to accept the challenge. Once things got started, it usually went one of two ways: The fling would continue for a few weeks and then cool off, a scenario that suited Dabs and was usually best for all involved. Or, the man would start to get attached. When that happened, the sport was gone, the challenge was missing, and the fun would turn into a burden. It never ended well, but it always ended on her terms. And whether the end came with her lover groveling or threatening, eventually word would get around about the last guy that got a little too possessive, and they would go without a fuss.

When she took up with Eric, Dabs was thinking that maybe it was time for a change. She hadn't met too many nice guys over the last ten years, none that she could stomach anyway, but he seemed pretty smart and he had a good sense of humor. He was ambitious, that was a plus, at least he had a plan for moving forward. While the bar business had been good to her, its earning potential had topped out years before. She'd given up cocaine almost entirely outside of the occasional pick me up that helped her get through late nights of doing the books. She was still young, only in her early thirties, she wanted more. He pitched the idea and she took the bait.

It had taken about three months for her to realize he didn't have the business savvy to pull it off. He had big ideas but didn't know how to execute. He was weak on follow through. She was getting bored and would have dumped a regular suitor. Things had stalled and it had been decision time, so she pushed things along. He needed a nudge here and there. Her part of the deal hadn't required cash, she could simply cut him off and move on if she wanted. It was still an option even now, but it was ultimately a pretty sweet deal if he could pull it off, so she had made the decision: Hang in there until the end, but help him along with a little push here and a little nudge there as needed.

The problem was that whenever things got a little tough he imploded. It made her sick. He'd come into the bar and order his usual and never pay now that they were "in business together". He'd sit in her bar, drink her booze, and whine like a little girl.

As she leaned against her locker, Dabs fantasized about her Muay Thai instructor. She was warming to the realization that she really did have a *type* and that Eric just wasn't it. She didn't want a change of type if that change meant accommodating weakness. And while she could afford to cut him loose, the deal was just too good. She'd already made the decision to see it through, manipulating him was simply her method of helping him execute.

When the phone buzzed again, the locker rattled and it caused her to jump. Irritated, Dabs snatched the phone up and saw that of course it was Eric. She threw the phone across the locker room smashing it against the cinderblock wall at the far side. Didn't he understand she needed her space? What part of *I don't want to have anything to do with you right now* did she not make clear? The explosive action of smashing her phone revitalized her. She grabbed her gym bag and headed out into the cool night air. Smiling, Dabs decided to make Eric buy her a new phone. After all, he was getting free drinks and great sex, she should get whatever she wanted.

Chapter 14

Robert arrived at the Chase offices early the next morning. He felt good. It surprised him. Every other time he considered reentering his old industry the emotional upheaval made him nauseous. For some reason, this particular morning was invigorating. Maybe it was the change of pace from the previous months, or maybe it was the excitement of getting back in the game. "Or maybe," he thought, "it was the fact that he had nothing to lose. No stake in the game, no dog in the hunt," as one of the gray beards used to say at Los Alamos. Whatever the reason, he was enjoying it, and the world felt lighter and better with the prospect of helping someone else, while also using his knowledge and experience.

He didn't have an ID tag yet, that was coming in the afternoon, so the receptionist had to escort him to the coffee pot, and then on to the conference room, where Val and Tom were already in discussions with another man. He waited outside the door until Val waved him in, where upon entering; Tom Lawson introduced him to Eric Pierce.

"This is the man I was telling you about just now Eric," Val said. Robert noticed how terse she spoke. She was different here than she was at dinner. "He will be helping us build the management structure at the plant. Where we need you is in the position we outlined. You have options, but putting you in manufacturing is not utilizing your talent where it's most needed. Now if you'll excuse us, we have a busy morning planned."

With handshakes and nods all around, Eric Pierce exited the conference room. It seemed to Robert that Eric was not a happy man.

"What's up with him?" Val asked Tom Lawson. Tom just shook his head, looking perplexed.

With Robert glancing back and forth between the two of them, Val added words of explanation with a slight flavor of exasperation.

"This might be as good a place as any to start," she began. "Eric was Mark's Chief Financial Officer. With the restructuring, we split the company up into departments. Each Department Head is responsible for his or her own operation, supported by a Financial Analyst. The analysts will work for Eric, but the accounting structure we adopted comes from an independent firm that will perform audits."

"So, his position has been downgraded and he's not happy?"

"I guess," Val continued, "but I don't know why he's not happy. He'll make more money and have less responsibility. Isn't that everybody's dream?"

"Sometimes," Robert said, "It wouldn't have suited your husband though, would it?"

Tom Lawson raised his eyebrows.

"You're right," Val conceded. "But Eric is not Mark. Maybe it *is* a matter of power and control. That might explain some of the nonsense coming out of his mouth. But seriously?" Val looked toward Tom.

Tom continued the explanation, apparently for Robert's benefit. "Eric always fancied himself the financial wizard guiding Mark through the misty mountains. But Mark always made the decisions, and he always included Val in everything he did. I'm not sure Eric knows the extent of Val's continued involvement."

Val chimed in again, "First he's got this idea that I might sell the company, now he wants to be in charge of manufacturing? It makes no sense. He knows very little about manufacturing, and he's not an engineer. I can only guess. Oversight of the company was initially centered in our financial performance..." She paused trying to find the right words to explain the past and how the new transition was affecting the company structure. "What I'm saying is, Mark was focused on technology, but we let the numbers tell us what the market wanted. From that perspective, much of the financial department felt like they were guiding the company forward. It's understandable I suppose, but that perception was never reality. Mark always knew what the market needed, the numbers basically only told us *when* they would be willing to pay for new innovation."

That part of the conversation was fizzling out, so the three reviewed the agenda and began introducing Robert to each of the Department Heads, walking him through the overall management structure. Rachael was the last introduction and she offered to take him to lunch while Val and Tom went off to discuss more pressing business. Robert was thankful when Rachael offered to drive. His new clothes seemed to fit better when sitting in Rachael's BMW. And while his truck wasn't a total wreck, he was apprehensive as to her reaction. Welding was a dirty business and his truck looked the part.

"This afternoon we'll get your ID and then I'll give you a tour of the plant," Rachael told him as she sipped her iced tea. "Tomorrow we'll have informal chats with the manufacturing leads. Very clandestine." She winked.

"When do we conduct interviews?" Robert asked.

"I'm not sure that's how it's gonna go," Rachael told him. "I know that's what we discussed at dinner the other night, but I think Val has decided on a slightly different plan. She told me yesterday that she's narrowed it down to three people, a first, second and third choice. Her words. None of the other Department Heads have interviewed, Val has simply offered people the job she thinks they should have, and so far, everyone has accepted. Originally, she was thinking of conducting interviews, but I get the impression that she wants your opinion, and then and after hearing it she might decide without the interviews. One way or another, you'll be introduced to all three of her candidates."

Robert nodded but didn't respond as the food was being delivered to their table.

"I expected to spend a few months working with you on this, but it's starting to look like weeks, maybe even days," he began as the waiter left. "Everything seems so well laid out. I'm not sure I have that much to contribute."

"I think you'll be surprised," Rachael said. "The majority of the plant, those areas that handle high-rate production contracts? They run like a Swiss watch. Quality control is built into the process so there are only a few inspection points. The back corner of the facility that handles prototyping was originally under engineering domain. Mark was a hands-on manager for both design and prototyping. With the re-org, prototyping will go to manufacturing."

"Without reviewing the facility or talking with the people, right off the top of my head, I'd say that's a mistake."

"It may be," Rachael agreed, "but wait until you look it over. Having it under engineering creates its own set of problems."

"Like?"

"Like how do you make a seamless transition from a custom prototype into full scale production?" As it used to go, when Mark was here..." Rachael stopped and ate a little food. It seemed to Robert that she needed the time to compose herself.

"The thing that would happen," Rachael continued, "is the production guys would reengineer the whole thing, trying to make it simpler to build. Mark knew where changing the design would be okay, and where their changes would be detrimental. He ran a tight ship and everyone respected him. He was the boss."

"You don't think you would know what changes are detrimental?"

"I think I may. But I'm also wary. I don't have that much manufacturing experience. Most of those are guys have twenty to twenty-five years of knowledge. The one thing I know for sure? They're not going to listen to me." She smiled with self-depreciation.

"I get it," Robert said, putting his sandwich down for a little chew break, "we need a process for the handoff and a review team that can work together. You're right," he told her, "this *is* something I'm familiar with. We need to create a smooth transition to production. The government calls it *Producibility*, and in many firms it warrants a whole department. In my experience, however, it never functions well separately. It simply becomes the third head of a monster fighting for control." He took a sip of his iced tea. "You'll still need to step up and take charge. The minute manufacturing gets the upper hand is the minute you begin to lose control of your design. A whole project can get shot to hell all because of a few changes, usually the result of 'good thinking' on the side of manufacturing efficiency. So, think in terms of a *team* of people with a combined knowledge to make the changes, and in that team, you need allies that will defer to your engineering judgment."

"I know." Rachael played with her food a little while she spoke. "Val and I have already discussed that, and the structure is in place to give me final change authority. I just need to get settled in with someone I trust and respect. I don't want there to be any power struggles or bullshit games. Mark was a good friend, the *best* in fact. What happened is just not fair. I want things to continue smoothly. I want them to be better than before. We need to avoid all the petty conflicts that might, check that, *will* pop up. Mark's authority was complete. With him gone, it might get a little strange."

"Speaking of power struggles and bullshit games," Robert started to ask before taking another bite, "what do you know about Eric Pierce?"

Rachael gave him a quizzical look as he chewed his food. "Finance guy?" She shrugged and shook her head. "Nothing. Mark worked with him, but I never dealt with him. Why?"

"Just curious," Robert told her, "apparently he wants more involvement in manufacturing. I met him this morning. He didn't look happy and Val seemed irritated. Flustered, in fact. I was just curious if you knew how he fit?"

"No," Rachael said with a look of concern on her face, "I gotta let Val deal with that on her own. She's got a lot on her plate but I need to focus on doing the best I can in the position she's asked me to fill. I have no idea what's going on with finance. I was shocked when she asked me to take over engineering."

Chapter 15

"Would you listen to me for a change?" Eric was getting irritable. He had tried to explain but all she did was push back.

"I have been listening. I'm listening now. All I need to know is how you're gonna fix this. You're the financial hot shot with the big swinging dick remember? Certainly you've got a plan Hondo?"

"Knock it off with the John Wayne references."

Dabs kept her cool, staring at him from across the little table. They were sitting in the breakfast alcove of her condo just outside Corona Del Mar. Dabs preferred it when he came to her place. She hated his house; it was too big for him and cost more than she thought it was worth. He only bought it to further his image, he thought it gave him status. Considering his self-proclaimed financial prowess, she thought it proved him an idiot. Which was fine with her. An idiot with an over-inflated ego was easy to handle, she'd been handling them all her life.

"Look," he began to explain the situation again, wrongly assuming she hadn't grasped all the implications. "I'm still head of finance, but it's a different department now. Before, I had signature authority to move money around, now I manage a team of analysts that report on the rest of the company."

He paused waiting for questions. She had none this time either, but was starting to form one in her head that began with "you think I'm an idiot, don't you?"

"Okay, so find one of them and pull them into bed with us." Dabs shrugged her shoulders. "Doesn't this guy know anything?" she wondered.

"It's not that easy. First of all, each analyst also reports to his or her respective department head. I'd have to recruit one of them also. That's where the signature authority is held. One person would have to sign, the other would have to know where to bury the transaction."

"Yeah? So? It's called embezzlement. How is that different from before?"

Eric bristled at the term. "God she can be such bitch," he thought. He calmed himself before continuing, thinking "patience, maybe with patience I can make her understand."

"Technically before it wasn't embezzlement. The company is cash rich and I had the authority to make investments. When the options pay off, Chase ownership will make a profit."

She leaned her forearm on the edge of the table and leaned toward him in order to emphasize her next remark.

"Eric, you authorized transactions where Chase money became our money. Call it what you want, the law will call it embezzlement. When the options pay off you can slide out from underneath it and maybe nobody will be the wiser, but if they find it in the audit you'll get fucked in ways you never experienced in MY bed lover." She leaned back in her chair and took a sip from her coffee cup. Realizing it had cooled just a bit too much for her taste, she got up to freshen her cup.

"No, no, no. I was authorized to make investments and TSV is a legal entity, legally holding those options."

"Oh? So, Chase owns TSV?"

"Don't be a bitch. Chase will own a percentage, you know that."

"Now he's getting testy," she thought. "That's okay, a

strong dose of reality would be good for him, and he needs to stop kidding himself."

"Chase's equity is the capital investment. What did you call our percentage? Sweat equity? I haven't seen you break a sweat yet lover. I can hear the argument now: Your lawyer will explain how you conducted a legal transaction for Chase, buying into this investment opportunity. The prosecutor will show how the capital invested was 100% Chase and that the equity portion they purchased was only 20% of a company owned by you, the person authorized to make the investment. That's an 80/20 dilution of funds my friend. It's a classic case of you taking Chase assets and making them your assets. Tell me again how you didn't break the law?"

Now he was fuming, she could see it in his face. Taking advantage of the moment, she walked calmly back to her seat smiling at him all the way. She knew it would cause him to boil over. It was just so easy to fuck with his head, and that was a reflex action she couldn't control.

"Look," he began.

"Oh my god!" She cut him off. "You're going back into *'let me explain'* mode. I GET it! You're the one that's got his head up his ass!"

"What do you want me to DO?" he barked at her.

"Tequila Sunrise on the Veranda my ASS!" She snapped back. "You thought this was gonna be a cakewalk? Let me tell you buster, I've run my bar for ten years. It's never easy. You gotta fight to keep your position, otherwise someone will pull the rug out from underneath you when it's least expected. First, they cut you off from the liquid assets. You thought you were gonna end up running the place? Well, apparently you were not heir apparent to the throne! And a buy out? What were you thinking? That would take months, maybe years, to complete. And what were you going to say when they uncovered your little *'legal investment'*? No lover, our only shot was to put you in the driver's seat. The only way to do that is to upset the status quo so they've got no choice but to put someone in the captain's chair that can steer the ship through the stormy weather. Sometimes you gotta create your own opportunities"

His face was red and he was staring at her, but he wasn't speaking.

"Finally," she thought, "maybe he's starting to see it for what it really is! What a moron!" She gave him time to calm down and gather his thoughts.

"What do you expect me to do?" Eric began, "the way she's organized the company I no longer have access to investment capital. The only other areas that process funds are payroll and manufacturing. If I could get into the manufacturing side I could set up another cash flow source, but she already said no. You know I'm upside down in my house. If I leave Chase I can cash out my equity position there, but it's not enough. And then I'd have no income. I'd have to find another job, which I can do, but it makes things much more difficult. You however, have equity in this place, and you have equity in the bar. I think it's time for you to step up."

"Tell me about this guy that's taking over manufacturing," she said, ignoring his comment.

"All I know about him is that he's got the experience she thinks they need. He's got a rocky background. You can Google him. It goes back a few years, but there's still some information on the net."

"Do you think you can get him into bed with us?"

"I don't know! How would I do that? That's insane if you ask me! You're compounding our problems, you're not helping!"

Again, she let the comment pass, knowing he didn't have the nerve anyway.

"I'm a survivor," she said. "We're not gonna let this deal fall through, and I'm not gonna gamble away everything I've built. I'm not an idiot. That buy out idea was stupid; it put you on their radar. And you were wrong about how highly they thought of you. I still believe in the power of disruption. It creates opportunity. If their plans get a little shake up, who do you think will head up manufacturing?"

"What do you mean shake up?"

"I mean, if you're not in line to be the manufacturing

manager, who would be? Under normal circumstances that is?"

"I would expect Rachael, but she just became the engineering manager. She won't give that up. They'll bring in somebody else, just like they're doing now. What difference does it make?"

"What does she know about contracts?"

"I have no idea, probably not much. If anything, she knows about the engineering contracts, not the manufacturing contracts."

"So, genius, here's what I want you to do: Find a contract you can get your hooks into, double billing, whatever. Something middle of the road so it doesn't attract a lot of attention. Then, let's just say, that for some reason they need to put a temporary management structure in place. You're not gonna take over manufacturing, so start thinking clearly. Give them something that makes sense. Recommend that this Rachael step into the role temporarily, and then you volunteer to handle all the financials working directly with her. You've got one objective here so don't fuck it up! If you play your cards right, you can stay out of the spotlight. It set us up with another stream of funds, and you might actually be the hero this time rather than zero. No more of this 'I'm king of the world' shit, nobody's buying it."

"I'm not sure I'm comfortable with that. Double billing on contracts, that's fraud." He said it to her back as she walked to the sink to rinse her cup.

"Pull your head out will ya!?" She said, spinning around. "You crossed the line back on day one. The only way out for you is to keep feeding money into this bucket until we can exercise our options and cash out. If you want to pay Chase back on their investment that's up to you, but I'm telling ya, it's probably better just to bankrupt TSV and fold it up. There's no legal gain in cashing them out, in fact, it helps them build a better paper trail. And that path leads directly to your door lover. No, it's better to bury it once we're done with it."

"But if I cash them out, then there's no financial loss, and TSV can continue."

She leaned on the edge of the sink and let out a heavy sigh. Was he really that stupid? She corrected her thinking: Was he really that *naive?* And yes, apparently, he really was. She turned, leaned against the counter, and summoned her warmest most calming smile.

"Yeah, I guess you're right," she told him, trying her best to sound both sincere and disarming. "You keep track of all the funds that come from Chase, and when we pay them back, we're home free to build TSV." She smiled and looked past him through the glass doors of her patio and added, "Tequila Sunrises on the Veranda. I can't wait."

The company name had different meanings for each of them. Eric envisioned the bright sunny look of tequila and orange juice; while they sat holding hands watching the waves roll onto the beach. For him, their options on the beachfront hotel currently under construction would put them on easy street, and springboard his plan to become a heavy player in real estate.

For Dabs, she held the liquor license, which gave her a big piece of the hotel bar concession. It was her deed to the diamond mine, and the only real estate she cared about. Eric's big plan had been the door opener. It was the nut she hadn't been able to crack. Her name wasn't attached to that stupid company and she didn't care about his silly ambitions. When the options matured, she'd take her cut *and* the bar concession, then cut him loose. And if his big plan didn't pay off like he hoped, she'd still have the bar concession.

But, if it all fell apart, and it'd be just like the spineless bastard to lose his nerve and let it all implode, if it all fell apart she was *out*, and that just wasn't going to happen. TSV for her meant making drinks on the patio of her little condo on a lazy afternoon with some new lover. She had everything she needed in her life except freedom. This deal would change her future from going to the bar and checking the till every damn day, to doing whatever she wanted and watching the cash roll in. Eric's contribution to Dabs version of a Tequila Sunrise would be the blood red of the sweet grenadine.

He watched as she turned her gaze from the patio and

brought her attention back to him, making eye contact. She smiled and came toward him, putting her hands on his shoulders and gently kneading the knots out from his neck muscles. Her touch was telling him "everything's going to be okay" but the strength in her hands was a little disconcerting.

Chapter 16

Detective Earnest Derrota leaned back and put his feet on the bottom drawer that he'd pulled out from the side of his desk. If he put his feet on the top of his desk, his legs would start to go to sleep, his boss would give him side glances, and one of the bozos in the squad room would invariably sneak behind him and tip his chair off balance. He was clicking the capped end of a Bic pen between his teeth and thinking. The body shops had revealed nothing, the junkyards had revealed nothing, not that he expected they would since the vehicle involved had obviously driven away. A truck could have hit Mark Chase, and if it was big enough there might not be any damage at all. That Jobe guy drove a truck, but his involvement didn't make any sense. He didn't hear it when his name was called out the first time.

"Ernie, wake the fuck up!"

He looked to his left and saw it was the Homicide Commander who had called his name.

"Boss?"

"Rodriquez just caught another one, you're on deck. I need

your report on the gal that fell off that boat in the harbor."

"She partied too hard boss, nothing more to it, drank too much and fell over in the middle of the night. I've run everybody on the boat, there's no motive. Medical Examiner found nothin'. Just another case of natural selection among the rich and not so famous."

"Write it up! I gotta release the body." The man turned and walked into his office and closed the outer door.

Ernie put his feet back on the floor and closed his drawer. Punching up the case file, he made all the appropriate notes and checked all the boxes that would move the file to "closed" which would then cause it to show up on his boss's task screen. He liked their new computer system; filling out the old forms was a pain in the ass. As he walked through the details one last time to make sure he hadn't missed anything, he thought about the Chase case.

He was about to close that one also, chalking it up to random vehicular manslaughter, which would transfer it over to the traffic division. Nothing more would come of it unless they were lucky enough to tie the accident to a vehicle damage report. The odds on that were slim to none since the vehicle had left the scene. On a normal case, like the harbor drowning, there were people involved, witnesses, and folks on the boat. Normal procedure was to talk to everyone they could and run background checks. Match the time of death on the ME's report to people's schedules. Check on everyone's whereabouts, look for inconsistencies in their stories. Stuff like that. Accidents lacked motive, so most of their effort was routine and yielded nothing.

He hadn't done any of that on the Chase case. It wasn't required, but he just didn't feel right sweeping it under the rug, and he didn't like that fact that the wife didn't come down to the welding shop. "Probably a waste of time," he thought. But at the same time, if he didn't do a proper job and something popped up, it would make him look bad. It was a grind, but what the hell, he might as well be thorough. Ernie fished through his notes until he found the number, then he picked up the phone and dialed. As it was ringing, another thought crossed his mind: "Don't piss anybody off too badly." He made that mistake once before and it cost him two additional years getting promoted to Sergeant. When he first caught the case, he'd learned that the Chase name was connected to a lot of good will in this town. The last thing he needed was some highbrow hot shot making waves at city hall.

Chapter 17

"Here's the final report from the auditors. All the accounts seem to be in order, legally we've got all the assets differentiated and structured according to your wishes."

Tom Lawson placed the bound report on Valerie Chase's desk. She had spent the last few days signing legal documents and scouring through financial reports. The details of her and Mark's plan were falling into place nicely, and Tom had helped her select a new board of directors from within the company and the outside business community. Her role for the last ten years had proven to be very valuable in the contacts she'd made. Community leaders and the local business power structure were more than willing to help support and direct their company through this transition and into the future. It had been emotionally draining in recent weeks, reliving the grief of the previous months while she continued the process she and her husband had begun, but ultimately Val felt satisfied and was beginning to feel relief now that the end goal was in sight.

"How's the new guy working out?" Tom asked.

"Quite nicely I think," Val said as she leaned back in her chair and pondered the progress being made at the plant site. "Rachael is impressed. She and Robert make a good team. He brings all of his suggestions to her, they work it out together, and then he puts it all in writing. I've had two progress reviews with them since he started. His final write ups are constructed so that we can insert them directly into our company procedures, and then tailor them into desktop instructions and checklists. His experience in the government sector has been crucial, I think. What they're developing will meet all requirements of the International Organization for Standardization. ISO," Val shook her head at the acronym, "it's something Mark and I only had to deal with on a very limited basis with our commercial contracts."

"Will he take the job?"

"No, I don't think so. He's pretty adamant about not staying, even though he seems to be enjoying the work."

"Do you think it's a tactic for a better offer? More money in the eleventh hour?"

"No. I don't think money motivates him at all."

"You've been wrong before." Tom gave her a wink.

"Boy, have I!" Val agreed. "I still don't understand why Eric wants to stay. At first, he seemed so disappointed, even put off, but then he does a one-eighty and all I hear about is loyalty to the company, loyalty to Mark, yada, yada. He keeps asking questions about Robert and the work he's doing at the plant site."

"Yes, I know. He's asked the auditors for financials on our contracts and suppliers. I've instructed them to not disclose anything to Eric, and to direct him your way. Has he contacted you?"

"No. And I don't know why he won't go through channels. He's got analysts that report directly to him, he could engage them but he doesn't, he's got real control issues." Val shook her head in bewilderment. "He needs to sit back and learn to interpret the data from the structure of the financial controls we've got in place. I don't understand his need to touch everything personally, especially at the plant, his interest there was always minimal in the past."

"Well, whatever. I think I'm done here, unless there's anything else you need I'll be heading back to my office."

"No, I don't think so, thanks Tom."

"Hold on just a minute," she said as he headed for the door. Val spun in her chair and pulled a bound report from the middle of a stack on her credenza. "There's a couple of accounts I'm not familiar with," she continued, opening the binder to one of the pages she had flagged. Tom looked at the line Val had highlighted in pink. Then he flipped to another flagged page where he found two more highlighted accounts.

"I don't know," he told her.

"How do I find out?"

Tom closed the binder and opened it again to the cover page.

"These are the long-term growth assets." He turned past the second page of the executive summary and found what he was looking for; "Here is the person that compiled it. Give the firm a call and talk to the auditor. I'm sure they can forward you the prospectus and any other details you want to see." He was always amazed at Val's attention to detail. Even under emotional duress, her ability to focus was enviable.

When the phone rang, Tom waited with his hand on the door.

"Yes, put him through," Val told her secretary.

"Hello? Yes Detective, this is Valerie Chase, how may I help you?"

Tom watched as Val listened on the phone. He saw the changes in her face as her mind moved from analysis of the financial accounts, into curiosity about the phone call, and eventually into a look of dread and discomfort based on what she heard on the other end of the line. He came away from the door and sat down in the chair opposite her desk and waited.

Val looked at her watch and said, "Can you come by the house in an hour? Fine, I'll see you then."

She hung up the phone and gave Tom a look of disgust.

"What is it?" He asked.

"The detective that Rachael met downtown wants to talk with me about Mark's accident."

"Do you want me there?"

"It wouldn't hurt, I could use the moral support."

Before they left, Val made a call to the accounting firm and set appointments for the auditor to meet with her the following morning.

Chapter 18

Robert had just finished making notes on a set of technical requirements and was about to start creating a checklist. This would be his last detailed review, and after having separated each of the contracts into categories based on the similarity of their requirements, he felt ready to lay out a tiered structure for transitioning their products from design into production. The structure was easy for him and he found the task enjoyable. It was detailed administrative work that required an educated eye toward the technology. The tough part would be building an effective team, but that was Rachael's concern.

Following his first few days of orientation, he'd been immersed in the details of production. The contract reviews had taken a little more than two weeks, and he estimated that the write up would be a three-day effort, including a review with Rachael before making final edits. Wary at first regarding the size of the task, Robert was proud of their progress, and even happier that the overall time spent would be less than two months. He liked Val, and had become increasingly respectful of the company she and Mark had built. It was his intention to add real value and not window dressing. He decided that based on their progress, he would be able to perform a thorough review of their supply chain, and close out his effort for them at the two-month point.

"Want to go to lunch?" Rachael asked, sticking her head into his makeshift office space.

"Thanks, but no thanks. I haven't been by the shop for over a week. I want to see how Ken's son is doing, following his recent treatments."

"I want to introduce you to someone. He's a young guy. Very sharp, he works in Quality Control. I like him. He's a straight shooter."

"What's his background?"

"Varied."

"What's he doing for us now?"

"Final inspection."

Robert thought about it for a moment: Rachael had the tough task of building a team, but it was his responsibility to help her find people with the right skill set. She was the one that had to work with the team in the future, and having people she was comfortable with would be critical to their success. A good final inspector needed to have a broad understanding of the product requirements and insight as to the manufacturing weaknesses. An adequate inspector only needed to be able to read a blue print and follow procedure. If the guy wasn't good Rachael wouldn't have recommended him. But if the guy could point out stages in the production process that Robert already knew were a waste money, and better still, if he had ideas regarding manufacturing efficiency and cost cutting, he might be perfect for the job.

"Lunch it is," he told Rachael, deciding to go by the shop on the way home, "can this guy write?"

"I don't know really," she confided, "but he helped to tailor the procedures on a lot of our inspection points."

"That's a good start." Robert was hopeful.

It was early evening by the time he finally got to the shop.

Robert had worked with the procurement group all afternoon and walked out of Chase with a complete list of their suppliers. His plan was to match each supplier to the contract they supported. After that, he'd meet with all the production managers and look for any crossover efficiencies or opportunities for volume discounts. It was probably an exercise in futility, but he knew that once he'd looked under that last rock, he'd be done with his review, and could write up his final recommendations. He'd taken the list home and dropped it off before changing clothes and walking to Ken's shop. After spending the better part of the last month sitting at a desk, his leg was weak and his joints were stiff. He needed the exercise and brought his cane today just in case the round trip tired him out. A group of young men in their twenties were shooting baskets at the school and as he passed, one of them peeled off from his friends and walked alongside him.

"You need to be careful in this neighborhood," the young man said as they walked. Robert looked over and saw the momentary flash of blue in the gray eyes.

"I didn't think you were a messenger. Do I need protection?"

"If you'd learn to use that stick properly I may not be sent here so often."

A larger man with a beard watched them from across the street as they rounded the corner and stepped into a liquor store. The young man bought a pack of cigarettes and Robert bought a pint of Irish whiskey. The bearded man was gone when they left the store.

"This neighborhood isn't so bad," Robert said in the doorway. "What do I need to be careful of if God is watching over me?"

"Shit happens," the young man said as he lit a smoke. "Sometimes things happen for a reason, sometimes they just happen."

"Yeah, tell me about it. But it's all just a big fucking mystery isn't it?"

Robert saw the man's eyes flash to blue for a spit second then turn back to gray. The man smiled and nodded at Robert, then turned and headed back toward the schoolyard.

Joey was forming an intricate curve in a piece of sheet metal on the English Wheel when Robert walked into the shop.

"Hey old man," Joey said when he saw the cane, "haven't seen you around for a while."

Robert picked the cane up in his fist and shook it as he bent over and grabbed his hip with his free hand.

"Watch it with the old man comments sonny or I'll pick you up and flip you like a pancake!" He said with his best loud yet shaky "old man" voice.

Joey just smiled. Robert straightened and approached a set of frame parts loosely assembled on the ground.

"Customer decide what he wanted?" Robert asked.

"Yup. Full custom. We discussed a few details but basically he's turning me loose so long as I stay in budget."

"What's the plan?"

"Top secret, need to know. I could tell ya, but then…"

"Yeah, Yeah, I know," Robert stopped him.

"Can you weld this up for me over the weekend?" Joey asked, pointing to the frame pieces.

"Sure," Robert said. "Cut the chamfers and clean up the connections. It should go pretty quick. If you want anything special, make sure you mark it."

"I can come in early Saturday and help you jig it up and tack it. That way there's no confusion, and if you've got any suggestions I can hear em right away, but I've got to be out of here by noon and I'd like to get it into powder coat on Monday."

"No problem. Eight o'clock? Ken here?"

"Eight's fine. Ken's in his office."

Robert stopped and knocked on the doorjamb. His boss looked like he'd aged five years in the past week. Ken looked up and waved him to a chair.

"How's the boy?" Robert asked, taking a seat.

"Not so good," Ken admitted. "I'm not sure how long he can last. Chemo is really tearing him up."

Robert pulled the pint of whiskey out of his pocket and set it on the desk.

"You're a saint!" Ken said, spinning in his chair and grabbing two coffee cups. After looking them over, he handed one to Robert and told him "you might want to wash that out."

Wiping the cup with a paper towel, Robert set it on the desk as he returned to the chair. Ken poured him a shot and they toasted.

"To better health," Ken said raising his glass, "*fuck* cancer."

"Amen brother," Robert said, touching his cup to Ken's.

"You having problems?" Ken asked, pointing to the cane.

"No, not really. I'm just getting stiff from all the sitting. You know how it is," he said, nodding at Ken's desk between them.

"Yes, I do," Ken conceded, "how are things going at Chase?"

Robert gave him the run down, keeping it light, telling Ken of the progress they'd made to date, and when he thought they'd finish. Ken seemed to appreciate the chitchat; Robert believed it took his mind away from the more pressing family issue. Ken reiterated his support for Valerie Chase. On the walk home, Robert was overwhelmed with fleeting thoughts of sadness and anger. Some of them were bubbling up from old wounds, reminiscent of his personal experiences. Some were immediate, present day emotions. He knew Ken's pain, he'd lived it personally: Feelings of helplessness correlated to both the past and the present. There was nothing either of them could do, then or now.

Ken would be critical of himself, and wonder if he had doing everything in his power to help his infirm son. Robert knew that over time those questions would only increase in intensity and that Ken would carry his misgivings to the grave. Robert's anger was aroused, as was his sense of fair play. "At least I can help out with Chase," he thought to himself. "Why do You always dump things on people that they can do nothing about?"

Ken had told him that his wife Judy was participating in a prayer group. As Robert neared the little garage apartment, he decided on a course of action he hadn't tried in a long time. Cynicism had taken over during the last couple of years. Even though he was still a believer, Robert felt intercession was a joke. He'd become resolute that God did whatever the hell he wanted. Tonight, however, he was determined to try. He felt desperate and it was the only thing he could think of: Tonight, he decided he would *pray*.

Chapter 19

Val was sitting at her desk waiting for the auditors to arrive. Even after meeting with the detective the previous evening she was feeling confident. He'd explained that it was simply a matter of routine, making sure they'd covered all their bases. Now, putting the discomfort of the meeting behind her, Val focused on the fact that all of their plans were unfolding on schedule. She knew Mark would be pleased. She'd read the final report Tom had dropped off, and just as he had stated, all accounts were in order and the structure that she and Mark created together had been properly executed.

When the auditor and his supervisor had both been greeted and seated, she pulled out her list of questions. Issue by issue, she walked them through her agenda. Account by account, she would ask a question and the auditor would pull a file and show her the details. The whole process was quite satisfying and everything seemed to be in order. Turning to a flagged page, she once again spun the book around and pointed to a highlighted line.

"Tell me about this one."

The auditor once again reached into his files and retrieved a folder.

"Here is a list of the authorized transactions. The company is named TSV Capital Investments. According to the prospectus, the company was formed to manage both speculative and long-term growth opportunities for their investors."

Val looked the paper over, scanning for data that might reveal some clue as to how their money had been invested.

"I'm sorry," she said, "but this doesn't tell me anything. The only thing I can take away from this piece of paper is that we've given six hundred and eighty thousand dollars to this company. There is nothing here that tells me what we bought."

The auditor looked toward his supervisor, then back at Val.

"The transactions were all authorized," the auditor said.

Val stared at the auditor. Then she turned and looked at the supervisor, who immediately understood the gravity of his subordinate's error.

"Mrs. Chase," the supervisor hastily interjected, "our standard procedure in reviewing accounts of this nature is to verify the audit trail and insure that the appropriate signature authority was in place. This account is part of the long-term growth assets. Transactional authority for these assets was held at the highest level. We were instructed that for accounts having a net value less than one million, extensive due diligence would not be necessary."

"I'm not familiar with this account, can you tell me who authorized the transactions?"

The supervisor leaned toward the auditor and gently removed the file folder from his hand. He ran his finger down the list of authorization codes.

"It appears that Mr. Pierce authorized these transactions."

"Did my husband authorize *any* of the investment payments?"

"As I look at this list of transactions, no ma'am, it does not appear that he did."

"And who was it that instructed you regarding the level of due diligence?"

"That would also be Mr. Pierce."

Val went silent, more for her own thought process than anything else, but the supervisor took it as an admonition.

"Mrs. Chase," he began, "all of our audit procedures were developed with Mr. Chase, Mr. Pierce and Mr. Lawson. The process limits and levels of due diligence were established, reviewed, and signed off by all three gentlemen. That included your husband."

"Yes, of course," Val told him with a wave of her hand, "I was only thinking for a moment. Can you tell me the principals of this TSV company?"

"No ma'am, that's not in the file. It's a privately held LLC, a Limited Liability Company."

"I know what an LLC is," Val said, trying to contain her impatience.

"We can certainly identify the registered agent if not the managing officer. That's a matter of public record," the supervisor offered.

"Can you identify into what exactly we have invested over half a million dollars?"

"Not with what I have here in the file. We would have to dig a bit deeper, most likely we would have to call the company directly. They're not obligated to share financial data, but most companies will provide a complete accounting of their investor's funds upon request. We may need to go through formal channels." He made a point of establishing eye contact. "We may need to make the request through you Mrs. Chase. Like we mentioned earlier, when the net value was less than a million…"

"Yes, I understand," Val cut him off, her patience fading. She remembered one of Mark's little sayings: *When someone justifies their actions for the second or third time, it begins to sound like an excuse.*

"Before I ask you to increase the scope of your original task I need to get some idea of the potential impact. Can you provide me with a list of all accounts that have a net value of less than a million? I'm specifically interested in only those that have level one signature authority, and only those that had little or no due diligence performed."

"That should be a pretty short list. I'm sure I can have it for you tomorrow."

"Tomorrow will be fine, but I have a more pressing request, one that I'd like handled by the end of business today."

The supervisor straightened in his chair. Val felt it was important enough to push, and to push hard.

"This is something I'd like you to handle personally. I don't want it to get passed off to someone else, I don't want it to be discussed openly, and I want it as soon as physically possible. We can call your firm, right now while we sit here, I'm sure your boss will gladly clear your calendar if you believe you have a conflicting responsibility."

Both men stirred restlessly. Neither wanted to have their firm's partners getting a call from this woman. The supervisor spoke first.

"We will do everything we can to support your request Mrs. Chase, but what exactly do you need? If I don't have the authority, or the resources, to deliver what you ask, then we may need to make that call after all."

"Fair enough," Val said; "what I want is everything you can tell me about this TSV company without calling them directly. I want to know when they filed as an LLC, and who is listed as a managing partner. Any financial data, product data, news clips. Anything you can find." She leaned forward with her forearms on the edge of the desk, speaking as though in confidence. "My husband would not have invested over a half a million dollars in a company he was not thoroughly familiar with, so there has to be something in the record that explains who these people are and what we've invested in; does that make sense? Are these copies?" She asked pointing to the file. "Can I keep them? And I'd like a copy of the prospectus you referenced. And I'd like you back here in my office at five o'clock this evening."

"Forgive me Mrs. Chase, but can I ask why you don't just ask Mr. Pierce? Certainly he would have knowledge of this investment? After all, he authorized every transaction."

"No, you may not ask why," Val snapped, then immediately

decided on a softer approach. "I sometimes feel the need to educate myself on these matters outside of my management team," she told them. "My husband was very hands on, he was involved in all aspects of our business, and I need to step up my game. I'm hoping you can help me do that here today, on this matter specifically. I have a meeting scheduled with Tom Lawson and Eric Pierce, but I don't want to go into it and ask for help, I want to walk into that meeting having some knowledge of the subject matter and ask for their input. Certainly you gentlemen can appreciate the difference."

They nodded their agreement and as soon as the door had closed behind them, Val Chase picked up her phone and dialed Tom Lawson.

"I need you here at 4:45."

Tom Lawson knew her well enough; the tone of her voice contained no room for questions.

Chapter 20

"My GOD you're annoying! What's so interesting on that computer screen?"

It snapped Ernie out of his trance. He'd been concentrating on the greens and blues of the online form until his mind travelled *through* it and let his imagination take control. He realized, a bit self-consciously, that he'd been tapping the pen on his teeth and bouncing his knee against the middle drawer of his desk. He didn't know how long he'd been doing that exactly, but apparently it had been long enough to annoy his buddy sitting at a nearby desk.

"Sorry," he said, "lost in thought."

"Form's not that tough."

"Yeah, I know," Ernie said distractedly, "it's not the form, it's this Chase thing."

"Hit and run. Write it up and dump it."

"Yeah I guess. I don't know."

His buddy spun the chair sideways to face him and leaned over with his forearms on his knees, hands clasped together.

"What's up Ernie? You making something out of nothing

again?"

"Maybe," Ernie conceded. "Tell me what you make of this…" He grabbed his notebook and started flipping back.

"Guy gets killed on his motorcycle. We didn't catch it at first, but now it looks like a hit and run. Guy's rich, turns out he and wife are kind of a big deal. So, I'm thinking, better follow through ya know? Except, guy's wife doesn't want to talk to me, what's *that* about? Then I go see her at her house and she's got her lawyer there?"

"Geez. You think the wife's good for it?"

"No, not after talking to her. It kinda bugged me at first, but she and the lawyer are working the estate together, I guess rich people got a lot more things to deal with than you and me. Anyway, the lawyer made it clear she had little to gain with her husband dying. So, I ask her for a list of people ya know? Gotta start somewhere, at least ask a few questions? Turns out there are only a handful of people that were close to the guy, he was a techno-geek, kind of a loner, she was the socialite. So, I got this list of five people, all work at Chase, and she tells me not to see them on company time. I get it, don't disrupt the staff and all that, so no problem, I spend the afternoon and half the night running around and talking to people."

"Find anything worthwhile?"

"No. Just weirdness, that's all. So, I come back and run their licenses, check out their car registrations and driving records. I found nothing there either. I paid attention as I met with them, made notes on the cars they drove, see if there was any damage on any of 'em."

"Could've had a car stashed."

"Yeah, I thought of that, not likely, everything I saw matched up with DMV records except for a couple of holes. Can't find any motive, no hard feelings, everybody loved the guy. From what I can tell, every one of 'em thinks they'd be better off if the guy was still around."

"How 'bout his personal life?"

"He didn't have a personal life, guy was a workaholic from what I can tell."

"Everybody's got a past, everybody's got skeletons in their

closet."

"Yeah, but really, I mean, what am I doin'?" Ernie shrugged his shoulders. "I don't want to make a stink. Hard enough for people to lose somebody. I can't find any reason somebody would want to take the guy out, so if I keep pokin' around it'll probably just come back to bite me."

"So, what's bugging you? Write it up and put it to bed."

"There's some weird shit going on." Ernie shook his head. "I don't know, maybe it's office politics, I never understood that crap."

"Yeah, we know!" His buddy sat up and motioned all around the squad room. "Sugar coatin' it ain't your strong suit."

Ernie smiled, "Maybe I should just write it up."

"Okay, I'm hooked. What's the weird shit?"

"This ONE guy. Everybody paints me a picture of Mark Chase that's consistent except this one guy. He tells me there's a rumor that the man was having an affair."

"Not unheard of," his buddy offered.

"Yeah, 'course. But if it's a rumor how come only one guy comes up with it? And rather than acting contrite or ashamed, this guy seems kinda buzzed up that he's got the opportunity to tell me. He was just a little too happy about it for my taste."

"Did you run it down?"

"No. That's what I was thinking about when you so rudely interrupted my highly tuned intellectual process."

"Yeah, right, clicking your teeth and banging on your desk. Sounded like a train was coming through. Throw it back at 'em. Talk to the wife, confront the mistress, maybe you'll shake something loose?"

"Uh huh, and maybe I'll start a shit storm that blows right through this place. Besides, I'm not buying it. I already talked to the wife, the lawyer, and the alleged mistress. Remember the blonde that was in here? According to giggly-pants, she's the one was boffing the boss man. Can't find any telltale signs though, everybody's distraught, and it's a tight-knit group. The wife and the blonde are really close, it's like she's the daughter they never had ya know? Blondie considered both

106

the wife and husband to be mentors. She's really struggling, wife's really struggling, it's just an ugly loose end that doesn't tie anything together. If we got a murder, makes more sense for the wife to get hit. Unless it's jealousy on the wife's part, but I just don't see it, hell she promoted the blonde! Nothing to be gained for the two of them to be working together. Naw," Ernie concluded, shaking his head as he spoke, "my gut tells me this affair nonsense is bullshit."

Ernie always found it helpful to run through it out loud. It was like hearing the words rather than just thinking them brought them to life, putting flesh and bone on the concepts running through his notes and around his head. He made his decision.

"Naw, there's nothing there. I'm writing it up and putting it to bed."

Chapter 21

Tom had arrived punctually at 4:45. Val gave him a very short overview of what she'd discovered. The auditing supervisor arrived ten minutes late; he was alone.

"The young man that performed the audit doesn't have the background for this type of thing," the supervisor began. "He followed procedures, but I've taken over the accounts. I informed one of our managing partners that you've asked for some additional information, and that in the interest of customer service I was spending the afternoon pulling together the data you requested."

"So," he continued, "at this point, the audit has been completed and all procedures were closely followed. No one is aware of the details of your request, and from what I've found, there is no apparent impropriety."

Val was having a hard time containing her anger. This guy was going out of his way to cover his ass, but it was understandable. They had completed the job as it was defined, and Val hadn't yet enlisted the firm's help in performing a deep dive of the records. A lot of companies were managed via hallway conversations rather than facts, and in many ways, perception becomes reality. The danger he faced was that Val could pick up the phone, call a managing partner, and claim that their audit had failed to identify an impropriety. Even if the accounts were completely in order, and even if all procedures were approved and followed to the letter, that call would stir up such a fuss that the managing partners would take immediate measures, if only for show. People would lose their jobs, procedures would get rewritten, and opportunists inside the firm would pick up the rhetoric in an attempt to further their own careers. Changes would be made for the purpose of window dressing. It sucked, but that's the way it was.

"I am very satisfied with the work that's been performed," Val began gently. She needed someone she could work with closely. "And I appreciate the extra attention you've given to my request, Mr…. I'm sorry, I'm not sure I ever got your name?"

"William" he said, handing her a card.

"William," Val repeated, looking over the business card, "as I was saying William, I appreciate the extra effort. And rest assured that if we do find any issues with the account, I will gladly write a letter to your bosses telling them how your efforts helped identify and resolve the situation."

William smiled and nodded.

"Now, please tell me what you found."

"Well," William leaned forward and started pulling paper from an expanding file. "First of all, the company filed earlier this year, so there's no tax returns or year-end statements. They filed online through one of those convenience legal services, and they listed the filing service as the registered agent, so there's no record of the principals without digging deeper." He handed Val a copy of the Board of Equalization form. She looked it over and passed it to Tom.

"I have a copy of the prospectus, but it's nothing more than a statement of intention. There's no performance numbers or other data we can trace." He handed that to her as well.

"So then, I did an internet search. I went through a lot of

news articles and finally found one obscure reference to TSV Capital Investments, LLC. They are listed as one of the investors funding the renovation of a hotel in the downtown area." He put the article on the desk in front of Val and pointed to where he'd highlighted the name at the bottom of a two-paragraph article.

"That was the only reference to TSV. But I knew you'd be curious, so I went back and searched on the hotel and on the company doing the work." He started pulling paper from the file. "Here is an article on the planned renovation, it mentions the company and gives a little more information.   Here's another article listing some of the projects they've completed in the last couple of years.   Since the coastline is completely developed, these guys have been upgrading the older sections of the beach towns. They've taken the buildings up, creating second and third floors above the old cinderblock retail space. Originally, many of those old buildings had apartments above them, so access from the street was already architected in, it's really a brilliant plan."

He waited while Val and Tom looked over the articles, scanned the photos, and passed his research back and forth between them. When he could see them slowing down, he continued providing additional details.

"The renovation that TSV invested in, if that first article is correct anyway, is one block north of Main Street. It's on the corner and was originally two stories. A couple months ago they got permission from the city engineers to go up to a third level. They're putting a hotel above the retail spaces spanning the whole city block. It's up high enough to have a view of the ocean and the boardwalk. They're upgrading the look of the retail frontage, adding additional parking, and turning that street into cobblestone walkways that will eliminate cars and increase foot traffic to all the retail below."

William waited for their reaction, he was very proud of his research and assumed they'd find the investment as exciting as he thought it was. He was surprised when their reaction seemed nonplussed.

"It looks to me like Mr. Chase and Mr. Pierce have invested

in a very solid and very smart partnership that will upgrade the city infrastructure and no doubt make a lot of money." William wasn't trying to sell the idea; personally, he thought it was really very cool.

Val leaned back in her chair and looked at Tom. Tom was still sliding papers around on the desk, his brain connecting the dots. Val watched as the lines on his face traced a connection that travelled from confusion, to astonishment, and looked like it was starting to connect with anger. When he looked up at Val, his face had turned red and he opened his mouth to speak, she held her hand up stopping him.

"Thank you so much William," she said, spinning in her chair to face the accountant. "You have been a tremendous help. I believe that when Mr. Lawson and I meet with Mr. Pierce we'll know exactly what questions to ask." She stood and held out her hand.

William stood and shook her hand. "My pleasure Mrs. Chase. If you need anything else, feel free to call me directly, you have my card."

When he reached the door, he stopped and turned to them both. "I almost forgot," he said, reaching one last time into the expanding file. "I was able to put together the list of accounts you wanted to see; the ones that were under a million dollars and had level one signature authority? Like I thought, it was a pretty short list." He handed her the paper. "If you need anything else, I'm happy to handle any small requests, but if looks like more than a few hours I'll have to get a bid put together."

When the door closed behind him, Val turned to Tom and sat back down in her chair.

"Now speak," she said.

"What the *fuck*? I mean, excuse my language Val, but what the FUCK? Mark would never have approved this as one of our long-term assets!"

"I know," Val said, picking up the last piece of paper she'd been handed. Scanning the accounts, there was nothing she wasn't completely familiar with, making this TSV investment the only questionable account. "I think Eric finally found a way to get us into the real estate business."

"I know, but Val, if this is really what it's looking like it is, we need to call the police."

"And tell them what? We've put money into a blind investment? We don't know that he's done anything illegal."

"Yeah, okay, but seriously? I mean, he started dumping money into this thing when?" Tom began shuffling the papers on the desk until he found the disbursements. "Three weeks after Mark died! C'mon Val, we have to do SOMETHING!"

"Who do we call? Derrota? He's looking into Mark's accident. It looks to me like Eric saw an opportunity, and without Mark to stop him he ran with it. What department would handle this type of criminal investigation? If we call Derrota…" She shook her head and frowned. "God what a nightmare! There's no connection, but if we create one and the press gets ahold of it, well, this is just bad all the way around."

The question stopped Tom Lawson short.

"I don't know who to call," he said. "I'm not a criminal lawyer. But I can certainly make some calls and find out who to call."

Val leaned back in her chair and began to think out loud.

"Local police won't know how to handle it. And we can't really call them until we've dug deep enough to find some hard evidence of illegal activity. And what if there is none? And if he has done something illegal, as soon as we start asking questions the money will disappear. It's not enough money to interest the FBI, and I don't know how the Securities and Exchange Commission could address it since all the companies are privately held. I've heard about this type of thing happening before, a bigger company would quietly shut off the funds and bury it. They get their accountants to write it off and avoid the bad press. IF we can't prove anything illegal happened, and assuming we lose the money, the best we can hope for is to wind up in civil court. And the effect of that will only be to throw good money after bad. No, we don't know enough yet to call the police."

"I think we should dig into it." Tom offered. "This really pisses me off. Even if Eric didn't do anything illegal, we should fire his ass. This is way out of line, even for him."

"Cooler heads will prevail Tom. You make your phone calls, let's find the agency that has jurisdiction, but don't go any deeper than that yet. I'm gonna make some calls too." She picked up the printout of the renovation project. "I know these people." She turned to face him. "I mean, I don't *know* them, know them. But I've bumped into them at events. I think I can get us an appointment. Can you keep your morning schedule open?"

Chapter 22

Eric was halfway through his second scotch and soda. The first one went down quickly, and it had taken the ragged edge off his nerves, so he decided to slow down and savor the next few drinks. He took a sip and allowed the liquid to roll across his tongue and slide down his throat as he breathed in through his nose and enjoyed the smoky oak flavors. With a good single malt, you could identify peat in the aftertaste. There were those that recoil at the idea of adding soda to such a fine distillate, but those same snobs might add a dash of water to bring out the aromatic characteristics, so what the hell was the difference? He liked a little bit of fizz, it gave the drink personality; a bubbly personality. He smiled at his own cleverness. Setting the drink down on the table, he watched the glass sweat and the drips form. Lowering his head down to the level of the glass, he watched the bubbles jump almost to the rim. When the drink was fresh, the bubbles created a little shower of droplets that looked like miniature fireworks if the light hit them just right. But, ultimately, the fireworks would end and all that would be left was a ring of moisture on the table surrounding the glass. If he didn't use a cocktail napkin Dabs would get bitchy. The invading thought threatened to disrupt his comfortable and content mood.

"You gonna tell me my fortune?"

Dabs put one plate of potato skins and a separate plate of coconut shrimp on their table and sat across from him. He looked at her quizzically.

"You're staring at that drink like it's an oracle. Thought maybe you were gonna tell me something I didn't already know."

"As a matter of fact," he said slowly waving his hands above and around his glass, "your future is looking very bright."

"Really? How so Swami?"

"I've created another income stream. It will hold us for now but we've got to be careful, it's only a temporary solution."

"See? You fixed it. I knew you were a clever boy. Why only temporary?"

"I didn't have time to bury it deep enough. It's too visible, someone may find it and ask questions. I need to set up another shell, one that sounds more legit, reduces the risk of prying eyes."

"Set up two or three and leave them dormant. That way if anybody gets curious, all you need to do is shut the one down and activate one of the others."

"We shouldn't press our luck." That was what he told her, but actually he thought the idea had real merit. He held his opinion back, however, she was already acting like this was her show and it irked him that she was always telling him what to do.

"Whatever you say lover, you're the clever one."

He could never quite tell if she was being serious or condescending.

"Even if somebody sees it, don't those people report to you?"

"Technically yes, but I used to be able to shut it down. The reports go to at least two or three other people now. I can't keep a lid on it like before."

"Are you making any progress on getting more control over

the plant?" She really didn't understand why they called it *the plant*. To her, a plant was something green that grew out of the ground.

"Mmm-maybe," he replied, smiling and playing with his drink glass.

Dabs noticed Eric was acting very full of himself, his Cheshire cat grin irritated the hell out of her.

"What's that supposed to mean?" She wondered if once again he'd done something stupid. No matter how hard he tried not to, he seemed to always be calling attention to himself. She supposed that worked well in the corporate world, but the tendency certainly wouldn't help their plan any.

"Let's just say, Rachael's stock value may take a dive in the near future." He didn't think creating the rumor of infidelity would actually change anything in the transitioning management structure, but anything to drive a wedge between Val and Rachael would certainly give him a leg up. His smile faded a little bit. "It doesn't give me more control at the plant, but it might give me an edge with what I've set up. If nothing else it could buy us some time."

"What about the cripple?" She asked.

"Excuse me?" He was confused.

"The guy that walks with a cane, right?"

"I've never seen him use a cane. He limps a little bit sometimes, but I've never seen him use a cane."

"Trust me, he uses a cane. Plus, he's got other issues; he's got a sketchy past."

Eric stared at her. Sometimes the things that came out of this woman's mouth worried him.

"What?" she asked. "You told me his name, I looked him up on the Internet is all," Dabs told him with a shrug. He watched as she took a bandana from her hip pocket, folded it, and began to tie it over her head and behind her neck so that her hair would stay in a ponytail.

"You're the one that looks like a fortune teller with that black hair and the scarf. Why don't you tell me something that I don't already know?"

She reached across the table and grabbed his wrists and

pulled them toward her, turning his palms up as she pulled.

"Oh, look at this!" she said, stabbing the nail of her index finger into the meaty palm of his right hand. It hurt and he jerked back a little but her grip was strong and she held his arm in place. "This is your line of opportunity. I see a limping man stubbing his toe and you're the one that will come to the rescue."

She looked up and saw that his face was twisted, a cross between pain and trepidation. She smiled and tipped her head slightly giving him her most mischievous and seductive look.

"Oh? But what do I see here?" She switched hands to concentrate on his left palm, tightening the grip of her right hand on his left wrist. Bunching together all the fingernails of her left hand, she began to make gentle scratching circles on his palm, then she traced her nails down all four of his fingers, then back up to his palm and across his wrist onto the lower part of his arm, then back again. Flattening her hand, she caressed his palm softly and touched him with the pad of her index finger. "These are your luck lines," she said, tickling his palm, "it looks to me like you might get lucky tonight."

His face flushed and he shifted with discomfort. She knew exactly how to raise his heartbeat.

"What a sucker," she thought.

Dabs rose from the booth, went to his side, and ran her fingers through his hair. She stopped on the second stroke to grab a fistful and turned his head toward her. "Keep your eyes open for opportunity, lover. I've got to go to work." As she walked away she said: "Come by tonight." Then she turned abruptly and pointing at his glass she added: "And don't drink too much."

Chapter 23

Robert drove to the plant early the next morning and scheduled what he assumed would be a series of "short meetings" with each of the production managers. As it turned out, each manager was responsible for at least three contracts, and with each set of questions they'd brought a different team into the meetings for support. His set of "short meetings" turned into one long marathon that took them through lunch and appeared as though it might go late into the evening. At two o'clock he was seeing faces for the second or third time, and it became apparent that many members of the production teams were getting tired of being pulled off the job to answer the same questions on a different contract.

He'd learned enough, and decided that continuing the inquisition would not win him any popularity contest. In the interest of fairness and goodwill, he cancelled the rest of the afternoon and took the opportunity to review the material "stores" and the receiving docks. Selecting a random handful of suppliers for a spot check on a couple of long running production contracts, he met up with the logistics manager who gave him a walking tour of their receiving area and stocking procedures.

"It all looks pretty tight," Robert told the inventory manager, "can you tell me what's going on with this one?" Robert pointed to an account that was fairly new and seemed to have a large number of recent transactions.

The manager looked at the account with a furrowed brow. Robert waited.

"I have no idea what that is," he said, "I don't think I have any inventory from them. Let me check the computer."

After a few minutes of tapping keys and switching screens the man confirmed that they had no receiving account under the name TSV.

"What do they supply? It IS an inventory account, right?" Robert asked.

"It's set up as an inventory account, but there's nothing in the system for the receipts module. Usually they send me the paperwork so I can set it up. Every now and again it doesn't make it here, so when we get a shipment I've got to backtrack it though accounting to get the details so I can complete it in the system: Gotta have both modules; inventory and receipts, otherwise it won't close transactions."

"How can I find out what they supply? Who do I talk to?"

"Accounting," the logistics manager said with a shrug, "the only thing we do here on the dock is make sure the receipts match what we have on the shelf."

There wasn't much more to accomplish in receiving, so Robert thanked the man, packed his things and drove back to Chase's main building. He had an appointment with Val at the house at five, and just enough time to gather his things before he left. Seeing Eric Pierce in the hall, Robert made a detour hoping he might catch Eric in his office before walking back out to the parking lot.

"Can you give me five minutes?" He asked, standing in the doorway and knocking on the jamb.

"I guess," Eric responded, a little put off at the interruption, "what do you need?"

"I was curious if you could tell me about this supplier?"

Robert put the list of accounts on the desk upside down for Eric to read and pointed.

It took a second for his mind to grasp what Robert was pointing to, but when it did, Eric's reaction took Robert a little by surprise.

"What are you looking into the accounts for?" Eric replied with irritation in his voice.

"It was just part of my overall review," Robert said with a shrug. He thought it to be an odd question, it was a manufacturing account after all, why would the finance manager get testy?

Eric took a breath and tried to settle down. His mind was spinning.

"It's a supply account. So?"

"So, I couldn't find any inventory. Do you know what they're supplying?"

"All the supply accounts transition to the plant from engineering. All my guys do is set them up."

"Okay. Who would I talk to about this supplier?"

"You say there's no inventory? That doesn't surprise me. Some of our stuff is long lead. It can take a few months sometimes to get a receipt. I wouldn't worry about it." Eric looked at his watch, then turned and began to work on his computer.

Robert took the hint and began to put his things away.

"I can hang onto that," Eric said, turning back to Robert from his computer. "If you want, I'll look into it."

The whole exchange was weird as far as Robert was concerned. Maybe the guy was just a little weird. He hadn't needed to work with Eric since he'd come on board. Either way, Robert had already put the papers in his bag, so he used his appointment as an excuse to leave.

"That's okay, I've got an appointment I need to get to, we can take a look at it together sometime next week maybe," Robert told him, checking his own watch and heading for the door.

As soon as he'd walked out, Eric Pierce was on the phone.

When Robert pulled out of the Chase parking lot, a flash in

his peripheral vision caused him to hit the brakes a little too hard and the truck jerked to a stop in the driveway. It was only a parked car, but it took him by surprise since traffic never came from that direction. Normally he would've pulled out of the driveway without stopping. "I gotta watch myself," he thought. He was beginning to rush everywhere and hadn't done enough driving in Southern California to be completely comfortable with the aggressive idiosyncrasies of the locals. As Robert turned toward the highway, a large man with a beard started up the parked car. It was a tattered old Dodge Intrepid. It followed at a distance.

By the time Robert got to the Chase home Rachael was already there. The hood was warm on her Beemer, and Robert was relieved, thinking that at least this time he wasn't too terribly late. Val was fixing them both drinks, and when Rachael answered the door Val called from around the corner offering to make him his customary gin and tonic.

They discussed progress over drinks and compared notes. Robert and Rachael informed Val of their impressions during the various interviews with the plant manager candidates. Robert outlined his thinking regarding a specialist team to transition their products from design to production. Key players would form a group with the managers of both engineering and production to create a transition plan according to his templates. After the transition was successfully executed, the same group would keep analytics on production efficiency and work together to resolve any issues that popped up. He also outlined his plans for supplier qualification and second sourcing of materials. Robert edified Rachael's input at every stage. Val seemed pleased with they'd accomplished.

"I wish you'd consider staying on," she said to Robert. "Rachael's for it, we were discussing the option when you rang the bell."

Robert's phone buzzed with a message.

"Thanks for the offer," he told them as he worked his phone to check the message, "but I really don't think…"

"What is it?" Val asked, seeing the change in his expression.

"I just got a text from the young man at the welding shop. Apparently, my boss there has a problem."

Both Val and Rachael sat silently with their eyes on Robert, so after a moment he continued to fill them in on the text.

"Ken, the owner of the shop? He has a son in treatment; I think I mentioned that when we first met. Apparently, there's been a setback and he, Ken, is at the hospital. I think what I'd like to do is go by there and see how the kid's doing. If Ken's gonna be out of the shop for a few days I should probably fill in for him and help Joey."

Val and Rachael were nodding slightly, but Robert could see that both their minds were busy analyzing the changes taking place at Chase.

"What I intended to do, even before this happened, was to spend the next couple of days writing this plan up in a process template. I can still put it together even if I'm helping Ken. I'll get a draft to Rachael, and after she reviews it, we'll do final edits and run it back to you for approval." He nodded at Val. "I think I can have all of my tasks wrapped up within the next ten days. That will give us enough time to close my contract by the end of the month."

Neither of them had much of a reaction.

"We can talk about my future then if you'd like."

That got a smile out of both of them. As he walked through Val's living room, the supplier accounts bubbled up into his brain and he pulled a Columbo move stopping at the door.

"I almost forgot!" He said, pulling the papers from his bag. Turning to Rachael, he asked:

"Do you know anything about this account?"

Rachael looked at it, frowned, and shook her head. "What is it?"

"It's supposed to be a supplier, but I couldn't find any inventory. I tried to talk to that guy, Pierce? He said all the production accounts are initiated out of engineering, so I thought I'd run it by you. That guy seems a little odd, but hey? Who am I to judge?" He said it with a shrug; Val heard the name and her ears perked up.

"I'm sorry," she asked, "what account are we talking about?"

Rachael turned and showed her the paper, holding it in one hand and pointing with the other.

Val's face went pale when her eyes caught sight of the account. The reaction wasn't lost on Robert.

"What's wrong?" he asked.

"You said you asked Eric Pierce? And he referred you to Rachael?"

"No, not exactly. He didn't refer me to Rachael. First, he got a little weird, kind of abrupt, he asked me what I was doing looking at the accounts. When I told him it was just a part of my review, he told me not to worry about it. He even offered to look into it himself, but since I was coming here I figured I'd ask Rachael. He told me all supplier accounts originate from engineering?"

"So, he didn't tell you specifically to ask Rachael?"

"No. He just kinda sloughed the responsibility onto engineering. It's an inventory account, but what I thought was odd is that it has no receipts. Neither Eric nor the guy on the dock seemed too concerned. It's a new account, they both thought the situation would right itself when they got a shipment."

"Did you tell him you were meeting with me?"

"No."

"Did you tell him you were going to ask Rachael?"

"No. But now you're making me kind of uneasy about the whole thing."

"I'm sorry," Val said after composing herself, "Tom Lawson and I are already looking into this account. You say this is a supplier to the plant?"

"That's how I ran into it." Robert pointed to the printout with the account codes, indicating the contract and material code.

"I'm so glad you stumbled across this," Val said, fixated on the paper. "Can I keep this page?"

"Of course," Robert told her as he repacked his bag and got ready to leave.

"I will address this with accounting," Val told them, "there's no need for either of you to bring this up with Eric. In fact, I'd appreciate it if you avoided the topic. At least until Tom and I are finished with our review."

Robert and Rachael both assured Val that they would forget all about it unless she asked, then they exchanged a glance between them, and said their goodbyes. Robert guided his truck down the residential street toward Newport Drive. On the corner stood a large man with a beard leaning against the stop sign. As the truck approached the stop, the man pushed off and began walking up Newport Drive. Somewhere in the back of Robert's mind a little bell went off that had a ring of familiarity. But the traffic on Newport Drive was typically heavy for that time of day, and all his concentration went into timing a break in the stream of cars so that he could safely enter the flow.

Chapter 24

The sun had almost set as Robert pulled into the hospital parking lot. The drive down the hill was lovely with the ocean gleaming in the distance and the sun turning orange as it sank into the horizon. The irony was not lost on him, that the majority of the people in Orange County would be grinding their way home on the freeway, and a select few were inside the hospital trying to find shelter from the dark clouds of emotion surrounding themselves or their loved ones, and only a handful would be enjoying the beautiful scene that occurred every evening along the pacific coast.

It was hard to find a parking space, but he finally snagged one at the far edge nearest the street. The walk to the lobby allowed him to loosen up enough so that he could enter the front entrance without limping. The admitting office was off to the left and information was directly in front of him with a line. Security had been implemented at most hospitals around the area, and visitors were expected to register before being allowed to roam the hospital's interior corridors. "Probably a good thing" he thought to himself. Standing in line, he wondered about "security" and if there really was such a thing. Security seemed to be a big deal everywhere, and yet, somehow there were still crazy people that found a way to bring guns and bombs into the unlikeliest of places and commit mass murder in the name of religion. Maybe security was a convenient lie? An outward show of security being the salve that covers an open wound giving the fearful a false belief that they were able to exert at least some control over their healing or their future.

Robert knew that life was far more fragile than we allowed ourselves to believe. He didn't like the idea, but the only way to resolve his emotions was to carry the thought that *all our days were numbered*, and that in spite of the lies we tell ourselves, control was a myth. He signed in and found his way to oncology. It didn't seem fair. Sometimes life was full of wonder, more often than not however, it just sucked. Walking the halls brought back a cellular memory that made his body hurt unless he pushed it away consciously. Passing intensive care, the same department where, a thousand miles away, he first woke from the accident to learn his wife and daughter had been taken, he was filled with anxiety that made him feel nauseous.

He stopped in the hall just before the nurse's station. Diagonally in front of him was a small waiting area and he recognized Judy, Ken's wife, from the photo on Ken's desk. He took a breath and regained his composure, and then he crossed the aisle and introduced himself. Judy was very cordial, thanking him for coming, but prattled on a bit about how it was unnecessary. She looked so tired, Robert offered to get her coffee and she accepted, allowing him to bring it and sit with her.

"Ken's in with him now," she offered, "Danny was doing so well. We thought the worst was over, and then this happened. I think the chemo is too hard on his system." She almost cried but kept it together. Robert just sat with her.

"I'm going to go back in and sit with him for a bit, then Ken and I are going to get some food in the cafeteria. Would you like to join us?"

"Oh, thank you no. I wanted to come by and see if there was anything you need."

"I appreciate that," she gave his arm a squeeze, "I'll let Ken know you're here."

After about ten minutes Ken came down the hall, his eyes were puffy and red. Robert stood as he approached and they shook hands.

"Coffee?"

"No thanks, I'm coffee'd out."

"How is he?"

"Doctors aren't acting hopeful," Ken said as they both sat.

"What happened?"

"Hell if I know. He seemed to be doing better. His spirits were up, his strength seemed like it was returning, normal cycle following a chemo treatment. It's not a fun process let me tell you. Anyway, we heard a thump from his room and when I went in there he was lying in a heap on the floor. We called the ambulance and they brought him here. They still don't know what happened."

"Well," Robert began, "I'm pretty much done at Chase. Joey texted and told me you were here. I told them I'd be working down at the shop for a bit and they're fine with that. So, take your time, Joey and I can handle it. If there's anything you need you've got my number. Call, text, whatever you need, let me know, we've got your back."

Ken nodded his head. Robert was afraid he was going to break into tears. Finally, Ken stood and shook his hand, and without a word he turned and walked back down the hall toward his son's room.

When Ken was beyond the nurse's station and out of sight, Robert leaned his head all the way back against the top of the chair. He closed his eyes and let out a heavy sigh. When he raised his head again, a Hispanic woman in her early forties was sitting in the seat that Ken had vacated. She turned to look at Robert, gave him a pleasant and knowing smile, and her eyes flashed from brown to deep blue then back again.

"God answers prayer," she said.

He bolted upright out of his chair and stared down at her

seething with anger.

"THIS is how He answers prayer?" He snapped at the woman.

At first, she seemed taken aback by his response, then her eyes flashed again and a calm, patient, loving smile came to her face. She almost seemed to glow.

"Please be careful when you leave here. You may be in danger."

"I've had enough of this shit Gabriel, tell Him next time to send me an email."

Standing at the truck, Robert didn't remember walking out of the hospital. He remembered turning his back on the nice woman. He remembered being so angry he couldn't think straight, and he didn't remember signing out of the visitors log. He couldn't remember walking the halls, or through the main doors, or across the parking lot. And he wouldn't have remembered, even if he had noticed, the large man with the beard sitting in the lobby.

But here he was, standing at the door to the truck, his key in hand. Robert unlocked the door, got in, leaned his head back, closed his eyes, and once again calmed himself down. "Don't have a heart attack," he said out loud, and then added, "and don't run somebody over." He started the truck and carefully backed out of the tight space. Pulling the lever down into drive, he maneuvered the parking lot and headed for home at a calm, sedate pace. The window was down and the sea breeze was still warm as it angled off his shoulder and blew across his face and neck.

The large bearded man had to hustle at first, and got worried that if he broke into a run someone would notice. At the pace Robert had moved through the lobby, and then across the parking lot, the man was certain he'd lose him at the light if he couldn't get to the car before the truck drove away. But then the truck had just sat there in the parking space. It was like the guy had seen him and was waiting for him to catch up. It made the bearded man a *different* kind of nervous. He wasn't used to this type of task. It wasn't his gig, and he was starting to resent the cloak and dagger shit. But he was supposed to find out where the guy lived, and how else was he supposed to do that? He had to wait outside the Chase manufacturing building since before lunch, and now he was starting to get hungry again. Hunger made him impatient and irritable. As he put the beat up old Dodge two cars back from the truck he was following, he began chanting to himself: "C'mon dude, go home, it's late, you're tired, you're hungry, don't stop anywhere else, just go home, no restaurant, no fast food, there's plenty to eat in your cupboard, it's late, you're tired, you're hungry, go home, watch some TV, take a load off, yeah that's the ticket."

Chapter 25

Valerie Chase and Tom Lawson were sitting in a conference room located on the fifth floor of a glass tower near a part of Irvine that had more parks per square foot than you would expect any community to approve. It was that kind of thing that won awards for the planners. Tom was standing near the window facing northwest. Passenger jets were crossing his view as they angled down toward the runway at John Wayne airport on their landing approach. To the left, he could watch as they touched down. To the right, off in the distance, were the rolling hills that separated the coastal communities from the Inland Empire. And spread out in front of him was the sprawling area named the Valley of Saint Anne by Father Junipero Serra back in 1769.

"I'm not completely comfortable with this," he told Val.

Val was sitting at the conference table with a file folder and a leather-bound portfolio in front of her. It was ten thirty in the morning and the only concern she had was whether or not they would serve coffee. It wasn't that she needed another cup, particularly, it was more her desire for the meeting to be casual and professional rather than guarded and defensive. The first few minutes would set the tone, and if it wasn't what she wanted, she knew how to force the change.

"I know, but we're doing this my way," she replied.

"We need to go to the police. A crime has been committed."

"We *will* go to the police, but not yet. It will be a long and messy road to prove that a crime was committed, and need I say expensive? The bigger issue at stake here, for all involved, is the implication of shady business deals. That would be far costlier and needs to be avoided. So, whatever we do, we do together."

"I don't like it."

"That's because you're a lawyer and not a businessman."

"Why am I here?"

"You're my wingman. I wouldn't have brought *anybody* else. You don't even need to speak, there's only two ways this can go, and when we walk out of here we'll know which way that is." Tom turned from the window where he was standing with his arms folded. Val smiled at him.

A team of three entered the room. They were all in suits, and they were all men in their late thirties and early forties. Ben Fallon introduced himself and the others.

"This is our chief of legal and this is our head of finance," he said indicating the men on either side.

"Thank you for meeting with me," Val said graciously.

"How could I refuse?" Ben smiled as they sat. Tom came around the table to take his seat next to Val. "A call from the mayor? You have some influential contacts Mrs. Chase."

"Friends of friends Mr. Fallon, and please call me Val. It took me longer than I expected to secure this meeting, but I'm very happy you agreed."

"My pleasure Val, and please call me Ben. How can we help you today?"

"Well Ben, let me start by saying I've done some research on your company. You've done some very impressive projects across the city."

"Thank you. We're very proud of what we've accomplished. And we have many more projects in the planning stages."

"There's one particular project I'm interested in, specifically, one investor in one particular project. I'm here to gather some information. You might consider it sensitive, and I want you to know that if that were the case, I would understand perfectly. It's not my intention to cause any of us grief."

Ben expressed his "concerned" face. Val thought he'd overacted, but as the leader of the company, she knew that his primary role was sales, so she was willing to let it go. Val smiled.

"I'm not sure I understand." The other members of his team looked bored. One was sitting very still and appeared intent on the conversation. The other was fidgeting his chair slightly from side to side. Val wondered if he was the type to spin in a complete circle during celebratory moments at board meetings.

"Your hotel project just off Main Street? You have an investor that we need to discuss. There may be questions of impropriety."

The chair fidgeter stopped moving. The head of legal leaned his forearms on the conference table. Ben Fallon didn't change his position or his expression. No one spoke.

"We can't disclose investor information without their consent," the chief of legal said after an interminable pause.

Coffee hadn't been served, Val was hoping for better. It had taken three calls to get the right person. She'd had to explain more than she wanted for her contact to agree, but after understanding the situation, a number of additional calls were made that resulted in this meeting. There was a lot of money at stake and possibly a few good reputations. She guessed that maybe their guarded attitude was a good sign, indicative that her shared details had not been spread across the telephone trail.

"Yes," Val said, "I understand. This situation is possibly even more delicate than you could imagine." She leaned slightly forward in the direction of her counterpart. "May we speak privately?" she asked Ben Fallon. "I'd like to share some details that neither of our lawyers would be comfortable hearing."

His curiosity was piqued, but he didn't show it. Tom

noticed that their eyes were locked together across the table. After a moment of consideration, he stood.

"Let's talk in my office," he said to Val, motioning toward the door and opening it for her. Standing in the doorway, Ben turned to the receptionist and said: "Would you please bring a pot of coffee into the conference room for our guests. And I'd like a cup too. Val?"

"That would be very nice, thank you," she answered, thinking to herself, "now the real meeting will get started."

"Gene?" Ben asked, still holding open the conference room door. "Maybe Mr. Lawson would care to learn about some of our recently completed projects?"

The head of finance nodded and reached for the credenza, withdrawing multiple high gloss folders. The men were passing around aerial photos and project descriptions as Ben led Val toward his office. The conversation was stifled until coffee was served and the door had been pulled closed.

Val took a sip of her coffee while Ben added two of those little cream cups to his, carefully pulling off the tops so as not to spill and placing them directly in the trash. He noticed that she was watching him carefully. "I usually do this in the kitchenette," he smiled a little sheepishly, "not at my desk." He gave it a little stir and took a sip. Satisfied, he tilted backward in his leather office chair and looked across the desk.

"Okay Val, what's up?" This time, the look on his face was honest concern. The question was casual, the tone much more intimate. This was what Val was hoping to achieve.

Val took a deep breath and let it out. She opened the leather portfolio with her notepad and removed the file folder that she'd slid inside as they had exited the conference room. She kept both on her lap.

"I know that one of the investors in your hotel project off Main Street is a company called TSV Capital Investments."

"We call it the *downtown project* internally," he shrugged, "just for reference."

"The problem is that TSV has invested money that came directly from Chase. And I can't find any records indicating our percentage of ownership."

Ben didn't respond but Val could see the wheels turning.

"And you're telling me this because? I would think you'd be speaking directly with the TSV principals."

"The reason I'm speaking to you is out of respect," she paused, knowing she hadn't given him enough information to connect the dots. "This problem concerns both our companies and I felt discretion was warranted. Our internal investigation is pointing toward embezzlement."

That hit home, she could see it in his eyes.

"I thought that possibly we should compare notes. If the paper trail is legitimate, I could fill the gap in our own financial statements and we could avoid any embarrassing misunderstandings that an official investigation might create."

Ben Fallon was completely engaged. His call had come directly from the mayor's office. They were still negotiating permits on half a dozen proposed projects. Not only could an investigation completely shut down the project, but the suggestion of impropriety could send all his conservative investors scurrying back away from the spotlight. They were operating behind the "Orange Curtain" and it had taken years to build trust within the community.

He leaned forward and picked up his phone.

"Can you please send Gene to my office? He's in the conference room."

He leaned back and contemplated the woman sitting across from him. She was very calmly drinking her coffee.

Chapter 26

When Robert rolled over to check the clock it was just after four in the morning. He was so tired from the stress of the previous day that when he got home from the hospital he went straight to his bedroom to relax for a few minutes. Hours had passed and he was still in his clothes; he hadn't slept well, and now he was too uncomfortable to sleep.

He got up and made coffee. Unpacking his notes, and the laptop that Chase had loaned him, he put them on the small kitchen table and hit the power button. As the computer came to life, he moved the straight-backed dining chair off to the side and rolled the armless frayed office chair over to the table. He couldn't work on a chair that didn't roll, and his butt would only tolerate sixty minutes or less of the dining chair before he was forced to get up and walk around. Knowing that the better part of the next few days might be spent sitting in that little kitchen in front of the computer, if he was going to be productive, he had to have the right chair.

By eight thirty that morning he could take no more. Satisfied with his progress, about sixty percent complete was his estimation; he closed the computer and took a shower. When he walked through the shop's bay door, Joey jumped up from whatever he was doing, held up his hand and yelled "whoa, whoa, whoa." Robert stopped in his tracks and watched from a distance as Joey pulled a tarp out from under the bench and covered up a major portion of his project so Robert wouldn't see it. From where Robert had been standing it looked like a bunch mismatched of bits and pieces laid out on the shop floor in rows.

"Now you can come in," Joey told him.

"What's all this?"

"The Triumph! The frame's been powder coated. As soon as my parts come back from the paint shop I'm ready to reassemble everything."

"You don't want help?"

"Hell NO! I want it to be an *unveiling*. You see it before hand; you'll just try and talk me into a whole bunch of new ideas. The customer and I've been discussing it," he winked at Robert, "I've got it handled."

"Whatever you say," Robert told him with a shake of his head. "Ken's not gonna be around for a few days. I told him we'd keep this place afloat. What needs doing?"

"How's Danny?"

"Not good."

They stood for a minute not saying anything. Joey just looked at the ground, while Robert scanned the shop.

"There's four new jobs on the shelf, and there's seven I completed. How 'bout you handle the invoicing and call the customers. We move those seven out of here and the bills are paid. I can get started on the new ones."

"You're gonna be running this place soon," Robert told him.

"If Ken will let me."

"He'll let you. He won't be ready to let it go right away. He's gonna need to keep up his routines, so don't push him. But eventually, he's got to back off, and when he does you're the one that'll take up the slack."

"If you say so."

"Keep the faith my friend, keep the faith."

By early evening they were done. It had been a good day. Six of the seven jobs had been pushed out the door, paid in full.

Robert had logged three additional work orders, and Joey had gotten two of the four about halfway complete.

"The old man will be pleased," Joey said as they pulled the door down and locked it in place.

"Don't expect compliments. His mind will be elsewhere."

Robert walked to his bench and packed his hummingbird flower sculpture into a box. Joey set the alarm and darted out the man door, Robert closed and locked it within seconds of Joey passing through.

"Taking it home huh?" Joey asked, motioning toward the box.

"Yeah, I got some paint at home. Still not sure how I'm gonna finish it. You be okay by yourself tomorrow?"

"You know it," Joey told him as he backed his car into the street.

"You got my number if you need me," Robert called as he drove away. A hand came out the window and gave him thumbs up.

When he was in the upstairs apartment over the garage, Robert put the sculpture box on the edge of the kitchen counter and stacked his papers and laptop into one pile. Moving the pile off the table, he place it on the floor near the power outlet and plugged the laptop in to charge, irritated with himself for not doing it earlier. He left the door open and went downstairs to the garage. Picking through his boxes was easy enough, there weren't more than six or eight to choose from, the problem was he'd packed them haphazardly and not labeled them well. Finding the right one, he hefted it and carefully navigated back up the stairs toward the open door. His knee was still unstable, and since he hadn't bothered to strap on the brace, he took his time. The last thing he needed was to fall down his own stairs.

Robert put the box on the kitchen table and extended the end leaves giving himself a few more feet of workspace. Unpacking the box felt weird. Artifacts from a previous life: A pair of shoes, a flashlight, a baseball cap from a minor league team in New Mexico, a pair of pliers and a couple of screwdrivers. There was an award from a professional conference he had attended. Near the bottom was the object of his search. He spotted a corner of the old wooden box that had his hobby paints. He had all different types and a variety of colors, and for a moment, he harbored the fear that they would all be dried up. He let the thought go, deciding that even if he needed to buy more, at least he could entertain his imagination tonight. He had been toying with the idea of creating an eggshell motif on the leaves of the flower petals.

The last item he had to remove before he could extract the wooden box with his paints was a rolled-up tee shirt. It was heavy when he lifted it, and curious, he unrolled into his waiting hand a 38 special Colt Police Positive. The gun was probably eighty years old and had a four-inch barrel. It brought back a flood of memories for Robert. He'd forgotten all about it, having purchased it nearly twenty years earlier from an older guy that worked at the company. For its age, the revolver was in great shape. The man that owned it previously had taken good care of the gun and the two of them had gone shooting together quite frequently over the years. When Robert's daughter became a toddler, he'd wrapped the gun into the shirt and locked it in a toolbox he kept in the garage. Robert broke the cylinder open and gave it a spin. The gun was clean, oiled, and loaded.

Many people in Southern California opposed gun ownership. For them, having a loaded gun meant you were probably a criminal. To Robert, a gun was nothing more than a tool, and for a tool to be effective it needed to be ready to use, and used with skill. Under the tee shirt next to the paints was a box of ammunition. Robert folded the tee shirt and placed it on the corner of the table and put the gun on top. He always took good care of his tools. Next, he removed the ammunition so he could more easily get to his paints.

Robert opened the old wooden box and sat down. One by one, he lifted the bottles of paint from the box and read their label, tilting each one slightly to see if the contents were still liquid. Separating them, acrylic from enamel, liquid from solid, he considered each color for worthiness and application: Flower or hummingbird.

Chapter 27

"Bring me your file on the downtown project."

Ben's eyes hadn't strayed from Val as he spoke to his head of finance. The man just stood in the door looking surprised. When Ben turned to him and raised an eyebrow. It was enough to send him out of the room.

"I appreciate you bringing this to my attention," he told Valerie Chase, "More coffee?"

"I thought you might. And yes, please."

This time he walked her to the kitchenette. Silently, they both filled their coffee cups. Val waited while Ben doctored his cup the same way he had at his desk. Then silently he led them back to his office where he closed the door behind them. Val knew his mind was spinning. This was a man who was quick on his feet, yet needed the time to work through all the nuances silently, in his head. Val imagined that he spent a lot of time in his office, pacing around, taking in the view periodically while the gears of making money turned in his head.

"We will both need to be careful as we discuss this matter. There's certain information I might not be able to share. And if what you say turns out to be correct, there may be details I probably shouldn't know."

"Indeed," Val said, "but if we do, in fact, need to go to the police, transparency might serve us both. A joint effort to right a wrong decisively puts both our companies on the same side of any question a good investigator is sure to ask. We would be seeking police support together."

"That might be the best path," Ben agreed, "but before we even consider it, I agree we should compare notes; in confidence. And then decide whether to bring our lawyers into the discussion."

Gene entered the office, handed Ben the file, paused briefly, and then left, closing the door on the way out. Ben opened the file and began paging through it, Val waited as he familiarized himself with the details.

"What is the dollar figure you uncovered on your side Val?"

"We came across a total of six hundred and eighty thousand dollars in our initial audit." She noticed that the number did nothing to change his expression. "Recently we dug a little deeper and found what looks like an additional one hundred and thirty thousand from a different account."

"Shit," was all he said.

She waited.

"Okay, full disclosure, no lawyers. I'll show you mine, you show me yours. Damn, this pisses me off, we work really hard to vet our investors."

She nodded.

"TSV is a holding company. There are two entities that were identified to us, there may be more but we don't have it. One of the entities, named EPC, has a two-million-dollar option on the hotel construction costs. It requires periodic payment to remain in force. The total payments we've received to date equal eight hundred and ten thousand dollars."

Val nodded while she processed the information. Then she added some facts of her own.

"We have an employee named Eric Pierce. The original transactions of six hundred and eighty thousand he had authorization to make, but we can't find any record of entitlement on our side, only the payments. The additional funds he had no authority to pay, and in fact, look to be out and out fraud. Is there anything in your files that show my company as having invested in your project?"

He was flipping through papers as she spoke, shaking his head as he did so.

"Nope" he said with finality. "And it looks like Eric Pierce is the only listed principal for EPC. Cute. Eric Pierce, probably the E-P part of EPC. All the money comes in as TSV but the original contract stipulates the options are under EPC and the other entity, listed as Dark Angel Enterprises, holds the liquor license under the name Dabria Kincaide." He looked up at Val. "That name mean anything to you?"

"Not a thing," she said, "not the person or the company."

Ben Fallon leaned back in his chair and began to massage his brow. He turned and looked out the window.

"This is not good," he said finally. "It looks as though Mr. Pierce has taken your money, put it in his own pocket, and used my company as his bank of convenience. This is going to cause me a real problem, and not just with this project."

"Tell me about the deal," Val asked.

He spun his chair around to face her again.

"Pretty simple really. A two-million-dollar option represents ten percent of the total costs on the property. Final appraisals are expected to come in at forty million. Once the hotel is operational, the options can be converted into an ownership stake or sold off. The liquor license was a concession of convenience: It sweetened the pot for TSV and didn't cost us a penny. To maintain the options, EPC has to continue to pay on demand during construction. This is the type of deal we only make with private investors as we prepare to break ground. They come and they go. Some of them convert; most of them sell and move on to another project. It's easy to sell the options once the hotel is operational because the numbers are solid. Initial values are always based on market estimates of the final finished project. As you can imagine, cultivating the good will of an investor is important to us. Somebody's gonna get fired over this I guarantee you. When the word gets out, I could lose half of my key seed money nest egg. This is gonna be a big deal."

"I've got an idea that might save us both a lot of money and grief," Val told him. "I have almost a million dollars invested in your hotel Ben. I've cut off the funding source, but if I go after the embezzler through normal channels I'm out that money, and you're still a million short. You'll have to find someone to make up the difference I assume?"

"That's a minor problem. I can find another million dollars. My main concern is, the minute this all comes out, through normal channels my project gets stopped in its tracks while the police sort through all the paperwork. The million dollars invested is only a pinprick, the fact that it's embezzled money, well that's an infection that will spread across everything I've got going right now. No matter," he said with a wave, "we can handle the fallout. Our war chest to fight legal battles is spilling over, we'll weather the storm, but it's not gonna be pretty." He shook his head in disgust.

"What do you think about this as an option... "He listened intently as she outlined her plan.

"Do you think you can pull it off?"

"If I can, we both win. If I can't, I will at least try to keep the information contained. When we go after Eric, it will only be disclosed that he embezzled money from Chase. We should be able to keep it from spilling over onto you, and if we can, his options will expire and you can close the file."

Ben liked the idea. He was weighing the potential issues back and forth in his head while she laid it out, and after running it a few laps around his brain, he made his decision. Picking up the phone for the second time since he'd met Valerie Chase, Ben Fallon summoned his head of legal to the office.

Chapter 28

Dabs had been waiting in the car for almost two hours. She saw him go in, confirming what she'd been told, that this was indeed his address. She thought it strange he'd be living above a garage off the alley in a rundown neighborhood, but whatever. She saw him come back down, and then hobbling with the box, he took forever getting back up the stairs. After thirty minutes she was changing her plan again, thinking on the fly, trying to decide how to stage her "disruption". The only thing she knew for certain was that this guy needed to be tripped up before his stumbling around Chase blew the deal.

"Damn cripple," she thought, "why can't he just mind his own business."

Thinking of her options, she'd already missed the opportunity to stage an "accident" while he walked to and from the welding shop. There were only a couple of places where she could get away with it and not be seen. She could wait until morning, but no telling when this joker might go to work. He'd left almost two hours later today than what she'd learned was his normal routine. And he might not even go there tomorrow, hell, he might get in his truck and head into

Chase to cause more trouble. He certainly had Eric rattled. She could barely get him calm when he called. And then he talked nonstop all night about "what was he gonna say" and "what were they gonna do" when the guy came back next week so they could "take a look at it together."

"Geezus I'm working with morons," she thought to herself. Eric should have gotten that piece of paper out of the guy's hand when he had the chance, then all he would have to do is jockey the accounts around into different names. "It's not that easy," he kept whining. And her bartender was turning out to be a wuss, telling her, "I don't like following people." The guy's got no problem beating somebody to a pulp, but ask him to get a little information and he gets jumpy? What was that about?

The truck was probably her best bet. Wishing she'd thought a little quicker, Dabs realized he could have had an accident on the stairs, and she could have helped that along if she hadn't needed to pee so badly. That opportunity had also passed, and now she was looking at the truck. If he got into an accident, it would sidetrack him for at least a day or two. No big thing, with no brakes he might rear end someone at a light. Or he might run off the road. Around here, that would mean jump the curb and hit a sign, or a retaining wall. No big thing. If he hurt someone, well that would just tie him up longer.

She had to go pee. Hopefully the old cripple was in for the night. If not, she'd miss another opportunity, but morning was probably better anyway since there'd be more traffic. Better that he hit another car than a street sign. Another driver would make a stink and the police would help with creating a delay. And if he didn't take the truck, no big deal, he would eventually. All she needed to do was give Eric time to step up and change the accounts. If he played his cards right. "Check that" she thought, he was too stupid to play his cards right. If he didn't push his luck. Then he might even be able to slide into a more favorable role at the plant. She had real doubts, even though that was Eric's ultimate goal, all she cared about was that he fixed the accounts and kept the money flowing. He was trying to maintain his career while he stole from his

144

employer. "What a joke," she thought.

Dabs pulled the car around the block and headed toward the coffee shop on the corner. If he were still home when she got back, she'd cut the brake line and go home. Cutting the brake line would require her to crawl around in front of the truck. And crawling around on the ground at that very moment would probably cause her to pee her pants. She laughed at the thought. "Eric was the pants pee'r, not her."

When she returned to her "stake out" spot in the alley, the light was still on in the little apartment and the truck hadn't moved. Dabs figured the old man was done for the night. It was too late for dinner; hell, it was probably past his bedtime. She got out of the car, pulling her knife from under the seat and holding it against her leg just in case there were curious eyes she hadn't spotted. There was nobody around. She leaned against the car door hard enough to hear the latch click and looked up and down the alley. "What a shitty neighborhood," she thought. "Why would anybody live here unless they *had* to?"

She walked carefully around the truck. There were no blinking lights on the dash, so there was probably no alarm. At the front of the truck she took another look around. "I'm invisible," she thought, "like a ninja." Dabs dropped to her haunches and peered along the inside of the front tire. The rubber brake line made a small loop just behind the drum. "This is too easy, gotta love Fords. I don't even have to get dirty." She rose up once again to check her surroundings. The truck was unlocked. Maybe even cut the seat belt partway? Naw, that might draw too much suspicion. She was changing her plan again.

She heard a noise from the window above, someone putting a coffee cup in the sink. "What a shitty place to live," she thought once again, and then it hit her: This was a "bad" neighborhood. Bad things happened in bad neighborhoods. The guy was old, he was a cripple, and he walked everywhere. Certainly, he'd be identified as a good target by the bad element in a bad neighborhood. The thought excited her. Actually, she felt a little turned on. She thought about her

Muay Thai instructor, calculating the optimal time to trade Eric in for the newer model. The whole ninja, martial arts vibe she had going was causing her to fantasize about her instructor. She was growing weary of Eric's lack of stamina. She made her decision: Cutting the brake line was out. Too many variables. She decided on a more direct approach to solving their problem.

This was getting exciting. To heighten the experience, she pulled a small vial from her pocket and snorted a little bump of the white powder. Dabs took a deep breath and thought "just like the old days." She felt invigorated, alive, and in total control. She bounced on the balls of her feet a little, stretching her calves, then carefully started up Robert's steps. One at a time, very slowly, she gently shifted her weight from side to side so that her body didn't cause the scrappy two-by-fours to make noise. "When you can walk across the rice paper and make no sound grasshopper..." she mused to herself, biting her lower lip and making sure none of the neighbors had a clear view. At the top of the stairs, she stood erect at the side of the door, her body in shadow. She looked around again; nobody had a view of the entryway. Dabs leaned slightly and tried the nob but it didn't turn. Her heart was pounding in her ears. "God what a rush!" she thought. It was now or never. She took one step to face the door, raised her foot, and smashed it through the brittle jamb.

Robert had chosen the paint colors he wanted, separating those for the hummingbird from those for the flower. He didn't have enough red for the flower petals, and since he needed to buy more, he used what he had to try some experiments. He'd taken a piece of scrap metal and painted one corner with brush strokes, in the middle he'd made little swirls, and on the end, he dabbed little blobs of paint. Setting the test piece aside to dry, he fished some broken eggshell from the trash, washed it, and dried it on a paper towel. He stared at it for some time, but it just sat there doing nothing and saying nothing. Finally, he wrapped the pieces in the paper towel and rolled the screwdriver handle over it, breaking the shells into a variety of sizes. He ripped a cardboard flap off the box from the floor and sprayed it with glue. Then he sprinkled the eggshell bits on it, and stirred them around until he had a mottled surface of eggshell. He stared at it some more, and still it refused to give him any ideas. About the time he decided it wasn't the way to go, he gave in and painted it anyway. "Might as well see what you'll look like," he told the cardboard. He was engrossed in the task.

Hunched over the kitchen table he carefully applying red paint to a flap of cardboard. His half-glasses partway down his nose, he was completely lost in his work. When the door burst open he jumped, dropping his brush and knocking over the paint bottle. He spun halfway around in the swivel chair, his hand coming to rest on the tee shirt.

"What the hell?" He said, the words blurting from his mouth involuntarily. "Who are you?"

She stepped into the light. She was tall, muscular, and completely dressed in black.

"I am the angel of death," she said. Her pupils were dilated, and in the shadow, her eyes looked completely black like those of a shark. Robert saw the six-inch hunting knife clenched in her right hand.

"I've met Azrael," he said, and brought the revolver up to aim center mass as he'd done in shooting drills so many years before, "and honey, you're not him."

He gave the trigger one long smooth double action pull and gun the jumped in his hand. The original plan was to point the gun and tell her to leave. Pulling the trigger seemed to be an involuntary response. It wasn't part of the plan, but then again, the plan had been improvised on the spur of the moment.

The explosion was deafening as it reverberated off the walls in the little kitchen. At 158 grains, the 38 special is a heavy slug, but it doesn't carry enough energy to propel a human body backward. The flash of burning powder came out the end of the barrel and also sideways from the front of the cylinder, filling the little room with smoke. The bullet hit

Dabria Kincaide square in the chest and immediately stopped her heart. Robert saw her legs buckle, and as she went down, the force of the slug from fifteen feet pushed her torso enough so that her back hit flat on the floor of his entryway.

He held the gun on her and blinked the smoke from his eyes. He expected her to move, but she didn't. "I am Barachiel," he said out loud. He knew he'd said something, but his ears didn't hear it, they were still ringing and all sound seemed muffled like someone was holding a pillow over his head. He stayed in that position for what seemed like a long time. He didn't really know how long. She still held the knife in her right hand. She wasn't moving.

Robert slowly turned his chair and set the revolver on the tee shirt. He felt completely calm. He stood, walked to the kitchen counter, retrieved his phone and his wallet, then walked back to the chair and sat. His eyes never left the figure lying in the darkness. He opened his wallet and took out Ernie Derrota's business card. He dialed the number, but before hitting the call button he made a few noises to make sure his ears were working.

The voice that answered sounded groggy and irritated.

"Yeah?"

"Detective Derrota?"

"Yeah, who's this?"

"This is Robert Jobe. I've just shot a person that broke into my home while I was trying to decide how to paint a welded sculpture I made."

"CHRIST ALMIGHTY! And you call me? Call 911! On second thought, I'll handle it, what's your address?"

Robert gave him the address and ended the call. As his senses began to come back to him, his hands started to shake so badly he could no longer hold the phone. He put it down next to his wallet on the kitchen table. Dabs had still not moved. The smoke in the kitchen was gone but the smell and taste of gunpowder still lingered in his nose and mouth. It made him feel nauseous. Robert's whole body began to tremble involuntarily and he yelled out loud: "Goddammit Michael! Where are you when I NEED you?"

Chapter 29

Valerie Chase picked up the phone on the second ring without looking at the readout. It was late morning and she'd spent the last few hours at her desk going over each account one by one, making sure that no stone had been left unturned. As it was, the only new account was the one Robert had discovered. All production contract material accounts balanced, the retirement and 401K accounts were being managed by a third-party administrator, and the long-term company assets showed no additional abnormalities. Val believed the situation had been contained, and if her meeting with Eric went as planned, the nightmare would end. She was pre-playing different scenarios in her imagination, deciding how to lead the discussion, and what direction to turn should the conversation veer off plan.

"Valerie Chase," she said into the phone. Val had picked it up out of habit. As soon as she had, it occurred to her yet again that she could have let it ring through to her secretary.

"Mrs. Chase, this is Detective Derrota."

It took a minute for the name to register. Val wasn't

expecting to hear from the police again.

"Mrs. Chase?"

"Yes, I'm sorry detective. I was in the middle of something and you caught me off guard. What can I do for you?"

"Well. I'm sorry to bother you ma'am. But I've got a Mr. Robert Jobe with me here downtown. You were the only person he could think to call, so I thought I would talk to you first, make sure you were open to take the call before I gave him back his phone."

"Is he in trouble? Is he okay?"

"He's still a little shook up. I guess you could say he's in a little bit of trouble, but I think it's gonna be okay. We were gonna give him a ride home but thought it might be better if someone picked him up. I don't think he should be alone right now, and like I said, you were the only person he could think to call."

"You're worrying me detective."

"Look, I'm sorry I called. We don't need to bother you with this, I can have a patrol car drop him at home."

"No no, don't hang up. Rachael was trying to reach him this morning. I'm sure she'd be able to come get Robert. Can you tell me what happened?"

"He was the apparent victim of a home invasion last night. He ended up killing a woman that owned a bar in Costa Mesa. We still don't understand what's going on with her yet. Mr. Jobe claims he doesn't know the woman. He says they've never met. We've had him here all night asking questions. I've tried, but I can't find any reason to arrest him. Now that the adrenaline's worn off, guy can barely keep his eyes open."

A little alarm sounded in the deep recesses of Val's brain.

"Detective, may I ask the name of the woman that was killed?"

"Yeah, sure, I guess. We've got everything we need so there's no reason to keep it under wraps I suppose. Odd name, lemme see... Dabria Kincaide. Mean anything to you Mrs. Chase?"

Val reached out and put her hand on the desk in an attempt to keep the room from spinning. It had the desired effect on the room, but she had yet to get her breathing under control.

"Mrs. Chase?"

"Detective Derrota."

"Call me Ernie."

"Yes. I… I will… thank you, Ernie. Can you meet me at my office around three thirty this afternoon?"

"I was planning to go home and go to bed Mrs. Chase. I've been up all night chatting with Mr. Jobe."

"I understand. Maybe you can get some rest before this afternoon and still come?"

"Mrs. Chase. If you have information to give me I'm happy to take it over the phone."

"Detective Derrota. Ernie. I recognize the name of the woman as being connected to one of my senior employees. I have a meeting with the man at four o'clock. If you can get here, I'll bring him from the meeting directly to my office where I will introduce the two of you. I won't mention this situation with Mr. Jobe to him of course. I assume you would want to ask him some questions?"

"Mrs. Chase, maybe you could give me this man's name now? That way I can do my job. I can be discrete, you don't have to be involved."

"I'm afraid I can't do that Ernie," Val told him in a very matter-of-fact voice. "And he won't be available until after I meet with him this afternoon, so really, I think it's best if you could come here." When Val didn't get an immediate answer she almost panicked. She didn't want to get into a pissing contest over the phone, nor did she want to upset a police officer. He might be motivated to come right away and disrupt her plans. Her instincts took over, manipulating the silence as best she knew how. "If you can't come I understand," she added quickly, "If we don't see you this afternoon I will call you in the morning, after you're rested, and give you his name." She hung up without waiting for his response and stared at the phone. Her heart was pounding.

The phone rang while she was looking at it and she jumped at the noise, even though it was expected. Val didn't realize how on edge her nerves were until that moment. On the second ring, she launched out of her chair and bolted to the door, telling her secretary that she wasn't taking any calls the rest of the afternoon. Especially if that caller identified himself as the police.

Chapter 30

Detective Sergeant Earnest Derrota slammed the phone down. It woke Robert up. Sitting on the chair at the side of Ernie's desk, he'd laid his head down while Ernie was on the phone and immediately nodded off.

"I'm fine, I don't need anybody to pick me up," Robert said, lifting his head.

"That blonde gal's gonna pick you up. Why do rich people think they can control the whole fucking world?" Ernie was more than a little irritated that Val hung up and wouldn't take his call. The words *obstruction of justice* was on the tip of his tongue, and if she would take his call she would hear those words first hand.

Robert didn't know what to think. He hadn't heard their conversation.

"I gotta go," Ernie said, checking his watch and standing. "Go back to sleep. She'll be here soon."

"What about me?" Robert asked.

"You're all right. Don't go anywhere. I'm not happy about this whole thing, but I'm not gonna charge you unless I find out you've been lying to me."

Robert put his head back down. At this point he really didn't care. He'd told the cops everything he knew. He'd never met the woman. He had no idea what was going on either. All he wanted to do was sleep.

Ernie took off, stopping to let the desk officer know that Rachael would come for Robert, and to wake him when she got to the station. The bar wouldn't be open yet, so he decided to go home, shower, and try to catch a nap. His intention was to go by the woman's bar early in the afternoon and see what he could learn, then head straight to the Chase offices and find out what the hell was going on. The extra time would give him a chance to cool off. He calculated that it would be slightly less than smart for him to go there now, in his present state of mind, but if the situation were different he would have gone straight to the Chase building. And if the woman continued to be evasive, he'd threaten to take her into the station. Probably not a good move politically, but he wasn't known for being politically correct.

They woke Robert when Rachael showed up; it had been less than an hour since Derrota had left. Coming through the station, they buzzed him out the front entrance into the lobby. Rachael looked worried.

"Are you okay? What the hell happened?

"I'm fine. What did they tell you?"

"Nothing! I got a call from Val telling me to pick you up here. That's all I know."

"I'll tell you in the car," Robert told her. They walked silently to the BMW. Once buckled in, Rachael turned to him without starting the engine.

"I'm working at my kitchen table," he told Rachael, "next thing I know this woman busts down my door. She's holding a knife and tells me she's the angel of death?"

Rachael just stared at him. He shrugged his shoulders.

"And you shot her?"

"Yeah," he said, a bit surprised at his own actions. "I really don't know how all that came together. I unpacked a box that had an old gun in it. I had forgotten all about the gun, that's not what I was looking for in the box, but I guess I'm glad I ran across it. She wasn't there for conversation."

Rachael shook her head and started the car. "You want me to take you home?"

"I guess, not sure where else to go. Let's go there first anyway, then I'll decide if I want to stay there or not."

She drove while Robert looked out the window. They didn't talk about it on the way. When Rachael pulled up to the garage, Robert was staring down the alley.

"What is it?" she asked when he didn't open his door.

"I've seen that car a couple of times," he said, pointing to the banged-up Dodge parked three lots away. "I swear I've seen it. A guy with a beard was driving. I saw it parked outside the Chase plant; it was on the street, not in the lot. Come to think of it, I might have seen the guy on foot up by Val's house."

They both stared at the car for a moment longer, then almost on cue their heads turned and they looked up at the door to the little apartment above the garage.

"You sure you wanna go up there?" Rachael asked.

"Might as well. Everything I own is up there, including my clothes."

They turned back to the car that was parked in the alley. "You've never seen it parked here before?" Rachael asked.

"Never," Robert told her, "and I would have noticed. It's not from this neighborhood."

"You go up, I'll join you in a minute. I'm gonna call that detective and tell him about the car."

Robert stood on the landing outside his entryway door and surveyed the damage. The doorjamb was broken. The door would close, but it wouldn't latch and it wouldn't lock. There was a lot of dried blood on the floor. He stepped over it and walked in a few feet. Things had been moved around, but nothing was missing. He felt bad for Ken. Putting this place back together was not going to be easy, and for some reason he felt responsible. This was the last thing Ken needed to deal with; it would only add insult to injury.

The spilled paint had dried on the table. His sculpture was on its side and his cardboard test piece was on the floor. The laptop was still plugged in; at least the police hadn't taken it. The computer contained most of the work he'd completed over the previous week. As he looked around, Robert started to feel sick. He walked to the table, picked up his papers and the computer, and packed them all into the bag. He left it on the table and went to the little bedroom and took a duffle from the closet. He packed the duffle with enough clothes to last a week. Mostly tee shirts and jeans. He left his newer dress clothes. As he exited the bedroom and moved toward the kitchen he saw Rachael standing on the landing. Her eyes were on the blood, then she raised her head and looked toward kitchen table, which was a straight shot to the back of the apartment from the doorway.

"Jesus Christ!" She said, turning her attention toward Robert as he stepped into view.

"I can't stay here," he told her.

"No kidding!" Was her only reply.

He passed the table and took a step into the little kitchen. From the lower cabinet, he pulled a thin plastic grocery bag out of a bag of bags, took it to the table and selected six of the little paint bottles from his collection. With the paint at the bottom of the bag, Robert threw in a couple of brushes, then carefully placed the metal sculpture inside, taking care not to snag the thin plastic with the rough edges of the metal. After inspecting his packaging job, he went back and got a second bag from the bag of bags and "double bagged" the original bag. As an afterthought, he picked up the cardboard test piece. It didn't look too bad, so he added that to the bag alongside the sculpture. It gave the whole package a bit more stability.

Robert pulled the strap of the computer case over one shoulder and the strap of the duffle over the other. He picked up the grocery sack and turned to Rachael.

"Let's get out of here."

"Amen."

She was halfway down the stairs before he got to the landing. He pulled the apartment door closed as best he could and put his things into the backseat of the BMW.

"Where do you want to go?" Rachael asked.

"Hotel. Take me down to Pacific Coast Highway. I need to see the water."

They drove north toward Huntington Beach. Robert selected a midrange hotel and booked a room. It didn't have a view, but he could walk across PCH and sit on the sand if he wanted. And from the room, he could hear the ocean if the traffic was light.

"What should I tell Val?"

"Tell her everything. I'm gonna sleep for a day. Then tomorrow I'm gonna finish my write up and send it to you. I'm more than half done with it. I would have finished it today if I hadn't been so rudely interrupted."

He smiled at her as they stood at the door to his room.

"Okay" she said hesitantly. She didn't know what else to say.

Chapter 31

Ernie Derrota was tired and grumpy. He'd had a shower, gotten about two hours of sleep, and now he had to hit the road again. It was not the kind of day he imagined when he went to bed the previous evening. Getting the call from Rachael became just another interruption in an already strange day. Backing his schedule up an additional thirty minutes gave him enough time to grab a much-needed cup of coffee and check out this "parked car thing" before going by the bar and then ending his day at Chase.

After radioing in the license plate, he sat drinking his coffee while he waited for the dispatcher to get back to him on the registration. Sure enough it was Dabria Kincaide's Dodge. Ernie took a walk around the vehicle, noting the crushed front bumper. He radioed back for a tow truck and took off for the bar.

The bar was open. It was five after three in the afternoon. He had no more than forty minutes, otherwise he'd be late getting to Val's office, and that was *not* going to happen. The bar was empty when he walked in and the bartender was setting up behind the counter.

"What time does the crowd start?" Ernie asked, trying to start up a cordial conversation.

The big guy behind the bar took a long look at Ernie and then glanced at the clock.

"About an hour," he said. The guy knew he was a cop and he made it obvious that he knew. Ernie decided to stop playing around. He took out his phone, and when the guy with the beard looked back up, Ernie took his picture.

"What the hell you doin' buddy?"

Ernie held up his badge and started in on the guy. He had forty minutes and figured if he was going to get anything, he had to hit hard and fast. He took out a notebook, more for show than anything else, but the effect was interesting when people saw him making notes on their responses. He threw his questions out in rapid succession. He wanted to get the guy talking, and the faster he was forced to form an answer, the more natural and honest those answers would be. This guy didn't look to Ernie like the type who would rehearse his answers, and whatever was going down had end abruptly last night.

"This bar is owned by a lady named Dabria Kincaide?"

"Yeah?"

"Is that Ms. or Mrs.?"

"She ain't married."

"Is Ms. Kincaide here at the moment?"

"No."

"Do you know where she is?"

"No."

"What kind of car does she drive?"

"Huh?"

"Ms. Kincaide's car. What is it?"

"Blue Dodge. What's this about?"

"What's your name?"

"Marty."

"You ever drive the car Marty?"

"No."

"You sure?"

"Why?"

"Do you know how the car got banged up Marty?"

"Hey look, she did that before I ever drove it."

"I thought you never drove the car Marty?"

"Well, almost never. Once in a while she'd have me take it to... do stuff."

"Can I see your driver's license Marty?"

"What for?"

Ernie took a step back from the bar and put his right hand on his hip, pushing his jacket back as he did.

"Listen Marty, I'm just looking for information, but if you're gonna give me a hard time I'll have to take you down to the station so we can continue discussing this matter."

"Whoa," Marty said with his hands up. "What's going on? I'll show you my license, take it easy."

"Is this your current address?" Ernie was copying the information into his notebook.

"Yeah."

He took out his phone and called it in for confirmation. When he hung up, he turned the phone around to show Marty the picture he'd snapped.

"I got an eye witness that I believe is gonna put you in that car. Anything else you wanna tell me Marty?"

"Hey, I didn't hit nobody, I'm telling ya, whatever she hit, she did it a couple months ago. I only drove the car when she sent me on an errand."

"Been on any errands lately Marty?"

Marty was starting to worry. He didn't know what to say. He'd already been tripped up once. He didn't answer right away.

"I'll take that as a yes, Marty. You and I are about to go for a ride."

"Hey, look, I drove it yesterday okay? She wanted me to follow some guy and find out where he lived, that's all. I brought it back here and she took off. I haven't seen her since, that's all I know, really."

"You a spare time private investigator Marty? You followed a guy to find out where he lived? Can I see your PI license

Marty?"

"Hey! She's a crazy bitch okay? I work for her, she tells me to find out where a guy lives I do it. Ain't against the law. Not like I could look him up in the phone book ya know. Ask *her* about it. I don't know nothin' about it. It's got nothing to do with me."

"Wanna tell me who you were following Marty? Maybe fill me in on where the guy lives?"

Marty absolutely did *not* want to tell him. In fact, he didn't want to be having this conversation at all. No telling what Dabs had done, she was so goddamned unpredictable. And now she'd roped him into it by having him run another goddamned errand in her goddamned car. He didn't see that he had much choice.

"I don't know the guy's name," he started. "She pointed out the guy's truck to me one morning. Then yesterday tosses me the keys to her goddamned car and tells me he works at some manufacturing place. Tells me to find out where he lives. Crazy goddamned bitch." He shook his head. "Really, that's all I know. You want to know more you're gonna have to ask Dabs."

Ernie hung his head and took a deep breath.

"You just ruined my evening Marty. I thought I was gonna be able to drink a beer and watch the game, and you pal, just ruined my evening."

Ernie made a quick call as he paced around the bar. He was running out of time.

Five minutes later, two patrolmen walked into the bar.

"Hi guys. Please escort this gentleman down to the station so he can give me a statement. I've got to take off, but I should be back there by five."

"HEY!?" Marty contested. "I don't know nothin'. You gotta ask Dabs. I can't close the place; she'll have my head. Can't this wait until she gets here?"

"I don't think you gotta worry about that Marty," Ernie said. Stopping at the door, he turned around and added "Crazy goddamned bitch is dead."

Chapter 32

Eric was excited. He hadn't heard from Dabs, which bothered him a little. But he hadn't seen Jobe around either, which was a relief, he wasn't ready to deal with that yet. And now, Val wanted him in a meeting. Maybe this was the opportunity Dabs told him to watch for? Val didn't tell him what the meeting was about, and she wasn't taking calls, so he really had no way to prepare. He grabbed a notepad, just to have something in his hands. He'd been anxiously sitting in his office for thirty minutes. At five minutes to four, he straightened his tie and headed for the conference room.

Val was nervous. Derrota hadn't arrived and it was already five after four. Maybe he wouldn't show. That would mean plan B. She was so hoping to execute on plan A. It was time to go, so she gathered her papers and walked from her office. On the way toward the conference room, she saw the receptionist accompanying a man and they were walking her direction. The receptionist pointed. As they drew near, Val realized it was Ernie. She was still a little wound up and hadn't recognized him from a distance; they'd only met the one time at her house.

"Detective Derrota. Ernie. I'm so very glad you're here, really, I am. It's very important that I speak with you. Would you mind waiting just a few more minutes? Would you like a cup of coffee?"

Before he was able to respond, she turned to the receptionist and gave direction to provide him with any beverage he preferred, and then she quickly walked off toward the conference room. The receptionist was to bring him there in about fifteen minutes according to the boss lady.

"What the hell," Ernie thought, "another fifteen minutes won't matter." And he desperately wanted coffee. He followed the receptionist and took his time fixing his coffee while trying to arrange and rearrange the facts bouncing around in his head. He wasn't looking forward to another late night, but talking to the bartender was going to be interesting. If he was lucky, he could wrap that up fast and still get home by around six thirty. He needed to show Marty's picture to Jobe. He'd have to find out where Rachael took him.

"Back to plan A," Val thought to herself excitedly, "this might work out after all." She got to the conference room ten minutes late and saw through the window that Tom Lawson and Eric Pierce were already there waiting. Sitting outside the door on a chair against the wall was a young woman with a leatherette pouch. "Perfect!" she thought, "I may have to take my admin out to lunch. Here goes nothing."

"Gentlemen, I'm so sorry I'm late, thank you for waiting," she announced as she pushed through the door.

"Eric, thank you for coming," Val said taking a seat directly across from him. As she arranged her papers on the table, Tom Lawson took a seat between Eric and the door.

"Of course, Val. What's up?"

"We have a problem. Tom and I were hoping you could help us."

"Whatever you need. You know that. What can I do?"

"Well," Val began, "according to these records," she placed her hand on top of a file folder, "you've been embezzling money from the company."

Eric was stunned. He wasn't sure he'd heard right. This was not what he was expecting. He looked at Tom, then back to Val.

"Val... I don't know what you're talking about."

"Yes, you do Eric, it wasn't a question. I really don't want to press charges." Val pushed a piece of paper across the table and turned it around so Eric could read it. "Tom and I were both hoping you could help us out. This agreement transfers all the funds from the shell company you set up. It moves those funds out of your name and back into Chase ownership where it belongs."

Eric looked at Tom. Beyond him, through the window and out in the hallway, the receptionist was walking their direction with the cop that had asked him questions about Mark. The guy was drinking coffee? Eric started to feel dizzy. The cop seemed to be eyeing him intently.

"Oh good," Val said as she jumped up, "I'll just be a minute."

She leaned out of the conference room door and asked the man to take a seat next to the woman waiting outside.

"That's a detective from the police department," Val said as she returned to her chair, "He's very interested in speaking with you."

"Val... Tom... I..." Eric was desperately trying to figure out how to sidestep this whole thing. They couldn't have the details, that would have taken legal action and he would have seen it coming. This had to be a ploy of some kind.

"This file," Val said, cutting him off, "contains all the documentation showing how you embezzled funds from our long-term assets. It also contains the documentation showing how you set up a fraudulent account to bill the company for material that was never received. Either you can sign that paper which will transfer the assets from EPC back to Chase, or I will invite the detective in here and give him this file."

Eric was looking over the paper. It made no mention of TSV, only the EPC options. How the hell did she find out about all the shells he'd created? It was drafted on the development company letterhead; they must have given it to her. Was that even legal? He couldn't believe what he was hearing and seeing.

"If I sign this you won't press charges?" he asked, tentatively.

"If we find that you've stolen other funds we haven't yet discovered, then I *will* press charges. But if this is everything, then no, we'll let the matter drop. Of course, you'll also have to sign this one too." She spun another sheet around and pushed it toward him. It was a letter of resignation.

"Val, I never stole that money. The investment is sure to pay off. Chase was gonna get every dime back."

"It's not a matter for debate Eric. No matter what your intentions may have been, you used your authority to transfer Chase funds into your own name. You hid those funds from us and then, WITHOUT AUTHORIZATION, you fraudulently billed against one of our manufacturing accounts to increase the value of your investment. If I give this file to the detective, he will no doubt seek charges from us as well as Ben Fallon's development company. I will help them all I can with the facts of the matter."

Eric picked up the pen and hesitated while he continued to look over the paper.

He turned to Tom and said, "If I sign this," he turned to Val and asked again, "you won't press charges?"

"Not if that's all of it. And as you can see, this won't affect your shell company or the arrangement you have with Ms. Kincaide."

Eric could barely breathe. She even knew about Dabs. He signed both pieces of paper. Transferring EPC shares back to Chase got him off the hook and left the TSV shell untouched. In the back of his mind, he was actually wondering if he could salvage his connection with Fallon by finding replacement money. His heart skipped a beat when Val went to the door, but she tapped the shoulder of the woman sitting outside and didn't speak to the detective.

"This woman is going to notarize your signature on the transfer. Are you sure there's nothing else I need to know about? The offer only stands if that's everything," Val said.

She was speaking a little fast, but she was the only one in the room aware of how hard her heart was pounding.

"That's everything," Eric told her. They were all silent as the notary went about her business. Val could tell Eric was deflated. His shoulders were hunched and he looked ten years older. He wouldn't make eye contact with any of them.

When the notary was finished, Val escorted her to the door. She handed the notarized signature page to her admin and gave instructions to have it copied and faxed to Ben Fallon. Then she turned and invited the cop into the conference room.

"This is Detective Sergeant Derrota," Val said, "I think you might have already met?" Val sat and Ernie followed suit, nodding at Eric Pierce.

"This is the man I was telling you about detective. He's been embezzling money from my company."

"VAL!?" Eric blurted in protest.

"Don't worry Eric, this has nothing to do with that." Val put up her hand to stop him and continued in a very amiable tone. "As I was saying detective, this is Eric Pierce, he's just returned to us all the money he stole. He's very sorry and I don't wish to press charges."

It was Derrota's turn to be surprised. He looked across the table at Eric who'd just turned beet red with anger. Wondering what the hell was going on, and afraid that this situation might turn ugly fast, Ernie put his coffee down so that his hands were free. His tired brain was struggling to get back on target.

"You had a question for Mr. Pierce, detective?" Val prompted.

"Yeah," Ernie began, collecting his thoughts, "do you know a woman named Dabria Kincaide?"

Eric panicked. Val just told the guy he'd embezzled money, she said she wouldn't press charges, and now he's asking about Dabs? His brain locked and his mouth shut down. "Who?" was all he could think to say.

"It's not a name you can easily forget!" Ernie's patience was wearing thin and he felt like these people in high priced suits were toying with him. The situation was pushing all his buttons. "DO YOU KNOW" he said in a protracted word for word manner, "a woman named Dabria Kincaide? She owns a bar in Costa Mesa? I've got her bartender in custody now. Easy for me to find out." Ernie was proud of himself, he'd raised his voice but he hadn't started yelling. He was on the edge of losing control.

Val put her hand on the file that was still lying on the table front of her, and tilted her head slightly looking at Eric.

"Okay, okay, so I know her. So what? She owns a bar. I go there sometimes after work."

"She's DEAD, that's what!" Ernie replied. His tone was not a nice one.

Eric turned white. The other three people in the conference room watched him; he looked like he might faint at any minute.

Val spoke first. She turned to Ernie and said in a very calm and even voice, "The man that identified one of Mr. Pierce's fraudulent accounts is a contract employee here. His name is Robert Jobe."

"That's it!" Ernie said, jumping out of his chair, "I've had it with this shit!" He walked to the other side of the conference table and lifted Eric Pierce to his feet. "You're under arrest," he said as he put cuffs on him and began to read the Miranda.

"For WHAT!" Eric nearly screamed. "VAL?"

"I don't know yet," Derrota said, then turning to Val, "you don't want to press charges?"

"No detective we do not wish to press charges. I was just hoping that Eric could shed some light on your other issue with Ms. Kincaide."

"You can't arrest me! I haven't done anything wrong!" Eric protested.

"Maybe not," Derrota said, calming his anger, "but we're gonna go down to *my office* and have a little chat. After that, I may have to let you go free."

"Why the handcuffs? I'll come without handcuffs. I haven't done anything!"

"With what I just heard, and this other issue which we'll be discussing, let's just call it professional courtesy. You know, crook to cop?" He turned to Val and Tom adding, "After I sort through this shit I may need statements from both of you."

"Anything you need detective." Val said with a nod. As she watched Eric being walked out of the conference room, she called out once again to the police detective. "Ernie?" When he turned to her, she held up a piece of paper. "Not that it has any bearing on his relationship with Ms. Kincaide, but I thought you should know that Mr. Pierce resigned before you came into the room. He's no longer an employee of this company."

Chapter 33

Robert turned his phone off and slept the whole day. Waking up once in the dark early morning hours, he put on a robe and stepped from his hotel room to listen to the waves on the beach across the street. There were only a few cars on PCH. He went back to his room and ate an apple, then went back to sleep. The next time he woke, the late morning sun was shining on the bed and his body was covered in sweat. He took a shower and walked to the beach. Sitting on the sand and watching children play in the waves calmed his spirit.

When he got back to his room, it had been straightened and the bed was made. He opened the laptop computer and finished writing procedures and checklists for the Chase Producibility Team. After one read through, he logged onto the hotel WIFI and emailed it to Rachael, then went back to bed.

He felt better on the morning of day three. Waking up famished, he walked to the corner for breakfast, taking a booth that had a view of both the pier and the shops along Main Street. He did some people watching while he ate. Locals and tourists alike were walking the sidewalks, the boardwalk and the pier. They were sightseeing and shopping, oblivious to anything outside their own bubble of perception. Back in his room, he unpacked the hummingbird and the paints, and immersed himself in his art. There was a banging on his door in the afternoon. The abruptness startled him, and for a spit second all the anxiety of his encounter with Dabria Kincaide came rushing back. He opened the door to find Ernie Derrota standing there.

"You scared the *shit* outa me," he told the detective, "the last time my door got banged on it wasn't trick or treat."

"Yeah, sorry about that. People are trying to get hold of you. You're not answering your phone."

"Have you come to give me a *serious beating?*"

"Naw, you're off the hook on that one."

"I turned my phone off," Robert said, inviting him in, "I guess I should turn it back on."

Derrota sat down on the little sofa to the side of the bed. Robert returned to the desk chair where he'd been working.

"Nice," Ernie said, pointing to the hummingbird.

"Thanks," Robert responded. They both sat quiet for a minute.

"You're off the hook on that other thing too: The trick or treater?"

"Good to know," Robert said, "ever find out who she is? He shook his head. Was?"

"Yeah, as a matter of fact we did, sort of. She's tied in with all this other shit that was going down." Ernie gave a wave of his hand as he explained. "She owned a bar in Costa Mesa. Her bartender was the guy with the beard you spotted. She had him follow you to find out where you lived."

"Why for god's sake!?"

Ernie shook his head in disbelief and smiled. "Apparently you stumbled on something that upset her plans. It took us a little while, but I think we got a pretty good handle on the story. We bounced the bartender off Eric Pierce." Now Ernie was fully smiling while he recounted the details. "Pierce was in a business deal with her and he was embezzling money from Chase to pay for it. We went back and forth between the two, telling one that the other told us something and vice versa.

Eventually bits and pieces started to fit together. I live for that shit, neither one of 'em asked for a lawyer, it was a blast."

Robert stared at the detective. None of it was fitting together for him yet.

"I'm glad you were entertained," Robert said finally when Ernie offered no further explanation. "None of that makes any sense to me. She was gonna kill me over something I didn't even know?"

"Yeah, sounds kinda weird from the outside lookin' in don't it? Imagine how I felt the last couple days! When you connect all the dots it sort of tells a story, but there's nothing concrete for us to pursue. The financial guy was embezzling money from Chase, he was in business with his girlfriend, she had the bartender follow you, yada, yada, yada."

"Did you just say 'yada, yada, yada'? I'm sorry but that doesn't really fill in the gaps for me! Do I need to worry? I don't want to meet anybody else with a hunting knife in their hand. You didn't give me back my gun!"

"Yeah, about that, you can come get it. All you have to do is sign for it."

"Detective?"

"Yeah, yeah, I know. I don't think you've got anything to worry about. I grilled the financial idiot for two hours, then I grilled the bartender for two hours, then I held them overnight while I tried to get some sleep. I talked to them both again the next morning. All the bartender will admit to is that he told her where you lived." He shrugged his shoulders. "All the financial guy will say is that they had a deal together where she used her liquor license to open the door to some hotel investment. The money he was embezzling was his contribution. Apparently, she was a bit erratic. Both of these guys were scared to death of her, and while they didn't like the fact that she was dead, they were a lot more forthcoming knowing that she was gone. Apparently, they were more afraid of her than they are of me."

"Anyway. I believe em. And even if I didn't, I got nothing to charge 'em with. The bumper on the chick's car lines up with Mark Chase's motorcycle frame. Sorta, kinda.

Bartender's got an alibi, so it had to be the woman, but there's no physical evidence I can use to tie it together. Can't place her in the car at the scene. I got nothin', but I don't see any threat from the other two. Financial guy gave the money back to Chase and resigned. They're not gonna press charges. We could go after 'em on conspiracy, but it's all circumstantial."

Derrota paused. Robert realized that he was listening with his mouth hanging open. He closed it and licked his lips, trying to bring enough moisture back to speak. Finally, he opened a bottle of water and took a drink. He offered one to Ernie, who took it and said thanks.

"So, let me make sure I've got this straight. You think she killed Mark Chase. And then she tried to kill me. We know she was in business with Eric Pierce. And you say he was embezzling money? Doesn't that tie it all together?"

"Not as far as a prosecutor's concerned." Ernie shrugged his shoulders at Robert again. "Even if Chase was pressing charges, there's nothing to tie Pierce to attempted murder. I think Kincaide was acting on her own. Both those guys totally lost it when we started talking murder conspiracy. Couldn't get them to shut up. Honestly, I think they were in the dark. The bartender could hurt somebody if he wanted, but Pierce? He's a weasel. He doesn't have the balls to commit murder. Like I said, we could press a jury based on circumstances, but..." Ernie shrugged again and trailed off the topic, taking a drink from the water bottle.

"Valerie Chase is not pressing charges? Does she know all the details?"

"She got all her money back from Pierce, that's why she's not pressing charges, there's nothing to be gained. The hit and run can't be proven, and even if we could prove it without a doubt, the murderer's dead. I didn't give her the details on the hit and run." He gave Robert a critical look. "I don't see how putting her through that would bring her any solace. Do you?"

"I guess not," Robert conceded after giving it long consideration. "I would suppose, that if you could tie the car to the hit and run, the embezzlement adds motive. But if the driver's dead, you gotta tie Eric to the event. And then you've gotta prove intent. Even without knowledge he's an accessory, but I guess it's a stretch huh?"

"You're a pretty sharp guy."

"Not sharp enough. You said I stumbled onto something? Maybe I could have stopped the train before it came to murder."

"It was all about the money. Pierce and Kincaide had the ball rolling long before you came along. According to Pierce, he was looking for ways to buy time until his investment paid off. He's so in denial it's pitiful. He claims the money was going back to Chase and that he was authorized to invest. Trouble was, he needed to keep the money flowing and Mrs. Chase mucked it up when she reorganized the company. He pointed the blame in every direction he could think of, eventually he started going in circles. He even tried to implicate Rachael, the blonde!"

That startled Robert. None of it made any sense.

"Ultimately, both those guys were afraid of Kincaide, and both described her as crazy. Why'd she act the way she did? What was she thinking?" Ernie held his hands up and spread his palms. "People do weird shit. If their scheme paid off, there were millions at stake, I've seen a lot worse happen over a lot less money."

Ernie pushed himself up from the sofa.

"Call your friends," he said as he walked to the door, "they're worried about you."

Robert wasn't in the mood to talk to anyone. He turned his phone on and texted everybody he could think of, telling them he was fine and that he'd contact them soon. Then he turned his phone back off and walked down Main Street looking for the Mexican restaurant that he'd been told served a killer margarita.

Chapter 34

When the call came to his cell phone, Joey snapped it up immediately.

"Where you been old man? We've been worried about you!"

"We who? You got a mouse in your pocket?"

"Ken's back dude. He went by your place and really freaked out. He seemed better after he called Mrs. Chase."

"Shit," Robert said, "I was hoping I could keep all this off his plate. You're holding the place together right? Why's he back? How's his boy?"

Robert was having breakfast and the thought of Ken walking into the bloody and trashed little apartment made him sick. When Joey told him, Robert had dropped his head into the palm of his hand and stared down at half eaten bacon and eggs. He had to close his eyes.

"Haven't you heard?"

"Heard what?"

"Danny's fine. Kid woke up hungry the next day, said he was feeling fine. Doctors checked him out and the cancer's gone."

"He's in remission?" Robert's head popped up out of his hand and he looked out on the sunny sidewalks of Main Street. People were milling about, shopping for souvenirs, eating gourmet ice cream, riding bicycles and walking to and from the beach in swimsuits.

"No, he's not in remission."

"I'm confused."

"They said it's gone. Not in remission. Gone. They can't find any trace of it."

"How's that possible?"

"Ken says Judy's calling it a miracle. He's been walking around here two feet off the ground. You believe in miracles?"

Robert was still gazing at the people moving about outside. They all had their personal battles going on, though you wouldn't think they had a care in the world as they tried to have a good time in the little beach town.

"On a good day I do," he told Joey, "and this is looking like a pretty good day."

"When you coming back?"

"I'll be around later this afternoon."

Robert hung up with Joey and texted Val. As he finished his breakfast, they arranged to meet at the house early evening.

The taxi brought him to his little garage apartment. It looked like Ken had tried to clean up. It was going to require some handyman work to get the door and the floors back in usable condition. Robert spent an hour doing what he could. He spent the next hour gathering his things and packing his boxes into the truck. When he was finished, he drove to the police station and signed for his revolver. Carefully wrapping it up in its original tee shirt rag, he packed it deep into one of the boxes. This time he left it unloaded.

When he pulled up to Ken's shop he saw a tarp-covered object off to the left that hadn't been there on prior visits.

"Hey there whipper shh-napper," he called to Joey in his best *old man* voice.

"Hey hey," Joey called as he came toward Robert wiping his hands on a rag. "You're looking well. And tanned. You been on vacation?"

"Yeah, I guess that's what you could call it. Is Ken here?"

Joey nodded in the direction of the office. Robert stopped in the doorway and knocked.

"Oh my God!" Ken said when he saw him. "I was afraid you were dead! Called Chase and got through to Mrs. Chase. She told me what happened. You okay? I'll have that apartment fixed up in no time, don't worry about it."

"Take your time," Robert said, "I got all my stuff out. I'm gonna head north for a bit."

Ken looked dismayed. Then the look changed to concern. "You're leaving?" he asked. Robert could hear the disappointment in his voice.

"Yeah. I need to get out of here for a bit. I may be back, you never know. Hey! Joey told me about Danny! That's great news!"

The change of subject worked. Ken launched into a joyous recollection of the last few days. First, they thought he was doing better, then they thought they were losing him, then he wakes up and he gives them a bit of hope, then the doctors give them the good news. "At first we didn't believe it," Ken told him, "We didn't dare believe it." He said he didn't think he or Judy could survive another up and down cycle if they held out too much hope and it turned out to be wrong. But little by little the doctors' tests confirmed there was no trace of cancer. The doctors told him it happens sometimes, but they couldn't explain it. "Judy says it's a miracle. I'm not sure what it is," Ken said, "but I'll take it."

"Every breath is a gift," Robert told him. "Enjoy your family. Enjoy whatever time you've got with 'em cuz you never know, one day they're here, next day they could be gone. Don't spend your life down here trying to make ends meet." Robert gave a little wave of his hand, motioning toward the shop.

"Gotta pay the bills," Ken told him.

"Let the kid do more," Robert motioned with his thumb toward the shop where Joey was banging on a piece of metal. "He's ready."

"How long are you gonna be gone?" Ken asked.

"Indefinitely." Robert knew where this was leading.

"You sure you gotta go?" Ken said, "You got a job here for life if you want it."

Robert smiled and nodded. "Good to know," he said. Then added, "The kid's ready."

"Speaking of which," Ken said, "he's got that Triumph all covered up. He's been waiting on you."

"Me?"

"Yeah. He worked everything out with the customer. Built the whole thing on his own. I thought it looked bizarre, but the customer went nuts, he loved it! Guy wanted to take it yesterday but Joey begged him to postpone delivery until he could show it to you." Then Ken added with raised eyebrows, "we made really good money on that job."

Robert smiled. "See? I told you. The kid's ready. Turn him loose and who knows? Maybe in a year they'll be filming a TV show out of this dump."

"Wouldn't that be something?" Ken said, "Hey! Lemme pay you."

"Nonsense!" Robert objected, "I've been working for Chase the last two months, they'll pay me."

"You've been keeping this place afloat. I owe you."

"I also trashed your apartment, and now I'm leaving with no notice. Let's call it even."

Ken smiled and nodded and closed his checkbook. Coming around the desk, he took Robert's hand and gave it a firm squeeze.

"When you head back this direction, there'll be a room waiting for you, and plenty of work for as long as you want it."

When they walked out of the office, Joey was in the middle of the shop bouncing up and down on the balls of his feet. He stopped and stood still as Robert put his toolbox into the back of the truck.

"You leaving?" Joey asked, looking distraught.

"Follow the yellow brick road," Robert quipped.

"Why you leavin'?"

"Because, because, because, because, because..." Robert sang back at him.

"Dude! You can't go! I got plans. You, Ken and me. You should see what I built!"

"I'm waitin' junior, all's I see is a tarp."

Joey pulled the cover off the Triumph and stood next to it grinning from ear to ear, he was beaming.

Robert thought it was disgusting.

Parked in front of them was a work of art, not a motorcycle. For Robert, it was also an abomination of transportation. For Robert, function translated to good design. Joey had hand crafted an aluminum tank that looked like a coffin. There were matching side covers for the oil tank and battery cover. The pieces were painted with a deep metal flake black that changed in the sunlight with glimmering shades of red and blue. The hardtail frame had been powder coated a dark shade of purple. The colors were matched perfectly, rather than clashing as you might expect. They played off each other nicely in the heavy afternoon sun. Chrome accents of flames and skulls were here and there providing highlights for the dark paint. The chrome handlebars were a T configuration, lifted off the triple clamps with flat black uprights, and angled slightly back. All the control lines were hidden in the bars and the frame. The titanium exhaust pipes that Robert had designed were properly discolored and blended well into the color scheme. The chrome springer front end was heavily raked forward with a small and narrow front tire. The back tire and custom fender was almost as big as the seat, which was the only item that Robert approved of, being a wide leather covered replica of motorcycles from the 1950's. The rear fender had a beautiful ridge in the middle that started out small behind the seat, rose toward the center, and then diminished again as it sloped down toward the street. At the peak of the ridge, the metal flared to accept an integral taillight with another skull cover intricately made from wire mesh. All the metalwork was hand made. Joey's work was master craft level.

Functionally, it would probably travel well enough in a straight line, but starting, stopping, turning, and all other functions that a motorcycle should perform well would be quite another story. It was, however, what all the custom shops seemed to be churning out and charging top dollar for these days. By doing all the work by hand, Joey was able to keep the costs down and also showcase his talent.

"Well?" Joey said expectantly, his excitement palpable. "What do you think?"

Robert tried to be careful with his delivery: "I'm an Engineer," he said, "to me, function is beauty and simplicity is elegance. This, this is art. Its basic elements are highly stylistic. The quality and workmanship are outstanding, but its sole purpose is to be seen. For me, a motorcycle should function well. This is kind of like a Jackson Pollock painting: It's either something you like, or something you don't."

Joey was visibly distressed by Robert's comment.

"Believe it or not that was a compliment," Robert continued, "look up Jackson Pollock if you don't believe me."

"It rides good, just not your style I guess?"

"Look, if you ride this thing, people are gonna notice it, and that's what you were after right? When I look at this, I think it should be sitting on a red carpet for people to walk around and admire up close. Put it on the street and the mundane will crowd it. The noise of banal repetition will drown out the statement you're trying to make. The best of paintings deserves to be displayed on a blank wall."

Joey was still rubbing his chin and looking critical toward his creation. Robert realized that his effort to give an opinion wasn't helping.

"Hey!" He said to Joey in the most uplifting and excited voice he could muster. "It's a beautiful piece of work! And the owner loves it, right?" He clapped a hand on Joey's shoulder and gave it a squeeze. "Good job!"

"So, you like it!" Joey beamed at the approval. "Wanna take it for a ride?"

"God no!" Robert exclaimed, then quickly added "Heaven forbid I drop it before your customer gets it! He should be the first to ride it don't you think? Honestly Joey? It's beautiful. You do incredible work young man."

As Joey walked away, Ken walked up.

"Ugliest thing I've ever seen," he said to Robert in a low

voice so as not to be overheard.

"Kid's gonna do fine," Robert told him, "he's dialed-in to what people want. Cut him a lot of slack and he'll not only make you money, he'll build a name for himself. If you're not careful, you'll lose him in a couple of years."

"If he does build a name for himself," Ken replied, "maybe I'll sell him the shop in a couple of years."

When Robert turned to look him in the eye, Ken gave him a wink and walked away.

Chapter 35

When Robert pulled into the driveway of Val's house, both the Land Rover and the BMW were parked near the door. Once again, he felt a little twinge parking the old truck behind them. He walked to the door carrying his grocery bag. He rang the doorbell and scanned the other homes on the hillside while he waited.

Rachael opened the door. The concern on her face faded when he smiled at her.

"I got your email," she told him as they walked through the living room. Val had gone to the bar to fix him a drink. "I liked your write up. We can dovetail it nicely into our current processes." Both women were dressed casually; Robert's clothes were grubby by comparison. He'd packed his new dress clothes and opted for his standard attire of jeans and work shirt before seeing Joey and Ken at the shop.

"I think you're good to go," Robert told her. "Whatever changes you need to make, you should make them with your team."

Val smiled as she brought him his gin and tonic. "How are

you doing?" She said with genuine concern.

"I'm fine," he told her, and took a sip. "Really, I am," he reiterated when she held his gaze, unwilling to accept his answer at first. "Thank you for the drink."

She led them to the patio where they sat and watched as the sun slowly started its decent into the pacific.

"Rachael and I reviewed the structure you recommended. It's a very good plan."

"I have every confidence in Rachael's ability to implement and execute," he told her.

"Are you sure you don't want to stay?" Val asked.

He took a long pull on his gin and tonic, set it on the table and looked across the horizon. With the setting sun, the rolling hills, and the blue Pacific Ocean in the distance, it was another beautiful day in paradise.

"I'm getting sick of this weather," he said, "I need some cloudy days and rain to get my attitude back on track."

They looked at him with a mix of concern and confusion. They'd never fully understand. Even with all that Val had been through, Robert knew that her path forward was to continue building what she and her husband had begun.

"I'm sorry you got mixed up in this mess," Val told him, "If I had any idea…" She just shook her head.

"Where angels go trouble follows," Robert said as he took another sip of his drink.

Val stared at him, the name Dark Angel Enterprises popping into her head. It was a name that would haunt her for some time.

"Shit happens," Robert said, "control is a myth. Gotta roll with the punches. Speaking of which, that detective filled me in a little, but I still really don't know why that woman came after me. Maybe I'm the one that got you mixed up in something." He shook his head in question and wonder.

"I'm sure that's not the case," Val said with conviction. "We don't understand it either, but our best guess, and mind you this is all speculation, is that Eric Pierce felt you were in the way somehow. Before your incident he was pushing me to give him more authority within the manufacturing structure. I never had any intention of doing that, and I don't know why he would think I would, but he did a lot of strange things that I don't understand.   He was in business with that woman.   I believe that she thought, maybe, moving you out of the way would open the door for Eric.   Seriously, I don't understand how some people think."

They sat and enjoyed their drinks, watching the sun get closer and closer to the horizon. The sky was turning from pale blue to an orange-red along the marine layer rolling toward shore from miles away. The tops of the hills on Santa Catalina Island were poking above the low offshore fog and were being highlighted with the light.   Robert saw Val turn toward Rachael.

"We could really use your talents at Chase," Rachael said on cue.

"Thank you," Robert told her, knowing he was really speaking to Val. "But you'll do fine without me. And I need to get away from here, for a while at least. I may be back," he turned toward Val, "You understand."

"Yes, I do understand," Val said with resignation. "If you decide to return, you have a job at Chase anytime you want."

"I've been hearing talk like that a lot lately," Robert said with a smile.

"Good people are hard to find," Val told him. "And you're a good man Robert Jobe."

She reached into her purse and pulled out a check.

"I have something for you," she said, handing it over.

"This is way too much!"   He told her when he saw the amount.

"Consider it a bonus," Val told him. "You helped rescue almost a million dollars of embezzled money."

"All I did was stub my toe on something buried in the dirt. You're the one that dug it up and set it right."

"Well, I've decided to continue funding Ben Fallon's downtown renovation projects. If all goes well, you're in line for a much bigger bonus than what you see here."

"Do me a favor and put that money to better use at the children's cancer research center down at the hospital. Also,

Ken may have some pretty hefty bills coming up. It would be a shame if he spent the rest of his life worrying over debt rather than enjoying what time he has with his son."

The sun was down. Just the tip of it poked out of the water, which had changed from blue to shimmering silver. Orange outlined the horizon and the sky above had gone from pale to deep blue. It looked like a painting. Their eyes instinctively rose, looking for the evening star. It would only be a few minutes until it winked into view.

"I wish you would consider staying," Val said. "I'll stop pushing," she added quickly, "it's just that you're very good at what you do."

"I'm good at it, but I've lost my passion."

"What will you do?"

"I'm hoping I'll find out." Robert studied the gin and tonic he was holding. "I seem to be stuck in stage two." When he looked up again they were watching him, and he realized he'd been talking more to himself than to them. He continued his thought for their benefit: "According to psychologists, there are five stages of grief: Denial, Anger, Bargaining, Depression and Acceptance. According to one counselor I was seeing, we bounce around as we process our emotions, but the goal is to get through to stage five. There're other feelings that coincide with the five stages," he looked up at Val, "but acceptance carries with it hope and reconstruction. I think you've made it to stage five. It's not a happy place, but it's a healthy place. There are things in my life that are a bit difficult to explain, but for some reason I seem to be stuck at stage two. Until I can work my way through it, I'll keep putting one foot in front of the other and move forward. My target heart rate is one beat at a time." He smiled at her, "What will you do?"

Val stared at her drink, took a deep breath, and let it out with an audible sigh. Her life was in order, but it certainly wasn't what she had expected. It wasn't what they had planned. "That's a very good question," she told Robert. "What's that old joke? If you want to make God laugh, make plans? *One foot in front of the other*," she repeated. "That seems to be my path also these days."

"I have something for you," Robert said, breaking the melancholy surrounding the conversation. He reached into the grocery bag and carefully extracted his sculpture. As he set it on the patio table both women gasped.

"It's beautiful," Rachael said. Val didn't speak. Her hands came up and she carefully touched it and rotated it slowly, examining every detail.

The hummingbird was painted in two shades of gray with brown highlights. There were traces of green around its eyes and tail. Suspended in flight, it was held in place by its beak, which was attached near the center of the flower. Robert had abandoned the eggshell finish. Instead, he'd polished the brass of the flower petals to an almost mirror finish, then coated them with a red tinted clear coat. The effect was a bright red flower that caught the light and reflected gold tones from the polished textured surface. The curved stem attached to a heavy base and aligned the center of gravity such that the whole thing sat nicely with the flower and bird suspended. He'd painted the stem and a couple leaves a dull flat green, with the base a mix of green and brown. The flower looked as though it was growing out of the ground. The colors of the stem and base were subdued; the effect was to highlight the bird and flower. The flower being the object that drew the eye, it allowed the viewer to appreciate the details of the attached hummingbird combination.

"Where did you get this?" Val asked finally after a lengthy examination of the sculpture. Rachael just smiled.

"I made it," Robert said.

Val turned to him, surprised. "You *made* this?" She said with wide eyes.

"It's a little hobby I have. The photograph I worked from was really much prettier."

"This," Val began and then paused, "This looks more like a vocation than a hobby."

"Well, I'm glad you like it." Robert stood and held out his hand. "It's been my pleasure to meet you," he said taking Val's hand, then he turned to Rachael and shook her hand as well, adding "and to work with you both."

They walked with him to the truck and said their goodbyes. They didn't press the issue of his leaving, but both expressed the desire to see him again soon, wishing him well and hoping for his speedy return.

Chapter 36

Robert maneuvered the truck out of the driveway and ambled down the residential street to the corner of Newport Drive. It was almost dark. Not completely dark yet, but the street lamps had come on and every other car was using their headlights. The traffic was heavy with commuters coming from the coast heading over the hill toward the freeway, and an equal number coming from the city heading home. "Another busy day in paradise," he thought. For a moment he wondered where "home" was for him. Sitting in his truck with a full tank of gas he felt a mixture of comfort and dread.

The traffic seemed interminable. He reached for the radio and hit the button preprogrammed for a jazz station. Louis Armstrong was singing, "It's a wonderful world." "Fuck THAT!" Robert said out loud and hit the button for the easy listening channel. A ukulele backed version of "Somewhere Over the Rainbow" was playing. "Better," he thought, and left it playing.

He darted into the flow, taking advantage of what only a seasoned Southern California driver would consider a "break" in the traffic. The guy behind him honked. Robert had accelerated hard up the hill and didn't think he had cut the guy off. The honk irritated him, and he instinctively raised his hand to give Mr. Honker the finger, then he thought better of it and waved instead. "You're a good man Robert Jobe." The words bounced around in his head. He really didn't know the definitions of good and bad anymore. Shit happened and you had to roll with it. Bad things happened to good people, and then there are the "wicked who get what the righteous deserve."

The business world was a jungle where every living thing was viewed as fresh meat. He'd lost his respect for running in the rat race. It was all just a big wheel where the faster you ran the more tired you got. "Meaningless! Meaningless!" Robert thought to himself, "Good old King Solomon. He was so wealthy that the Queen of Egypt fainted at the sight of his wealth. *All is vanity.* If old Sol didn't know, nobody did. I need to find my *passion.*"

As he headed for the freeway, Robert Jobe wondered if he was running from, or running to something. Whatever it was, it was something hidden and unknown. The only thing he really knew for sure, was that for some reason, it was time to go.

Made in the USA
Monee, IL
23 December 2020

53463626R00105